She Was A Stranger In A Strange Land, A Woman Desired By A King.

Suppose Zara gave in to Prince Rafi for one night, or one week, or… What would it mean, in the end? Did kings let women go, after they had loved them, or did they guard them jealously, not willing that any other man should ever have the power of being compared with the king as a lover?

Zara heard a clinking sound, and something that sounded like a horse whinnying. In sudden alarm, she lifted her head.

"Who's there?" Zara called, realizing she had been a fool to come wandering in the desert on her own. She ran light as wind toward the sheltering rocks. Damn the moonlight!

Then a black horse reared up in front of her. Out of the shadows, a body bent down and dark hands reached for her.

The prince?

She clung to him for safety; there was nothing else to do.

Dear Reader,

Why not sit back and relax this summer with Silhouette Desire? As always, our six June Desire books feature strong heroes and spirited heroines who come together in a highly passionate, emotionally powerful and provocative read.

Anne McAllister kicks off June with a wonderful new MAN OF THE MONTH title, *The Stardust Cowboy*. Strong, silent Riley Stratton brings hope and love into the life of a single mother.

The fabulous miniseries FORTUNE'S CHILDREN: THE BRIDES concludes with *Undercover Groom* by Merline Lovelace, in which a sexy secret agent rescues an amnesiac runaway bride. And Silhouette Books has more Fortunes to come, starting this August with a new twelve-book continuity series, THE FORTUNES OF TEXAS.

Meanwhile, Alexandra Sellers continues her exotic SONS OF THE DESERT series with *Beloved Sheikh*, in which a to-die-for sheikh rescues an American beauty-in-jeopardy. *One Small Secret* by Meagan McKinney is a reunion romance with a surprise for a former summer flame. Popular Joan Elliott Pickart begins her new miniseries, THE BACHELOR BET, with *Taming Tall, Dark Brandon*. And there's a pretend marriage between an Alpha male hero and blue-blooded heroine in Suzanne Simms's *The Willful Wife*.

So hit the beach this summer with any of these sensuous Silhouette Desire titles…or take all six along!

Enjoy!

Joan Marlow Golan
Senior Editor, Silhouette Desire

Please address questions and book requests to:
Silhouette Reader Service
U.S.: 3010 Walden Ave., P.O. Box 1325, Buffalo, NY 14269
Canadian: P.O. Box 609, Fort Erie, Ont. L2A 5X3

BELOVED SHEIKH
ALEXANDRA SELLERS

SILHOUETTE *Desire*®
Published by Silhouette Books
America's Publisher of Contemporary Romance

This book is dedicated to my niece
Jessica Sellers Stones,
that rarest of creatures—a poet

The poem "whisper of ambergris" as a retelling of the Persian poem by Unsuri was specially written for this book by Jessica Sellers Stones. Copyright 1999 by Jessica Sellers Stones. Used by permission.

 SILHOUETTE BOOKS

ISBN 0-373-76221-6

BELOVED SHEIKH

Look us up on-line at: http://www.romance.net

Printed in U.S.A.

ALEXANDRA SELLERS

was born in Ontario, and raised in Ontario and Saskatchewan. She first came to London to attend the Royal Academy of Dramatic Art and fell in love with the city. Later she returned to make it her permanent home. Now married to an Englishman, she lives near Hampstead Heath. As well as writing romance, she teaches a course called "How To Write a Romance Novel" in London several times a year.

Because of a much-regretted allergy, she can have no resident cat, but she receives regular charitable visits from three cats who are neighbors.

Readers can write to her at P.O. Box 9449, London, NW3 2WH, England.

THE BARAKAT EMIRATES

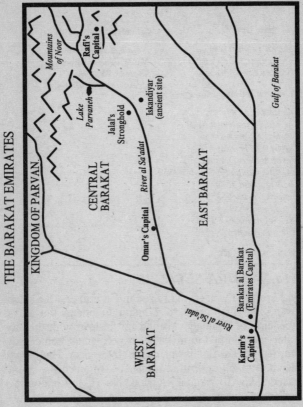

SHEIKH'S RANSOM, *Prince Karim's story*, April 1999
THE SOLITARY SHEIKH, *Prince Omar's story*, May 1999
BELOVED SHEIKH, *Prince Rafi's story*, June 1999

Available only from Silhouette Desire.

Rafi's Inheritance
The Sword of Rostam

———

To Prince Rafi's lot fell the Kingdom of East Barakat, a land of richly varied landscape, extending from marshlands at the seacoast, through the broad desert with its ancient remnants of civilisations long dead, to the broad flowing river called Happiness, and into the mountains, where his palace lay.

To him also was given the great Sword of Rostam. This fabulously jewelled and inscribed sword had, according to the ancient story, once been the battle sword of the great hero Rostam. Since that time, any King of Barakat who drew the sword in anger signalled to his people and to the enemy against whom he drew it that there should be no respite from battle until one or the other was vanquished. Once the

Sword of Rostam was drawn, negotiation was no longer possible.

Therefore a king must be very certain of his ground before drawing the Sword of Rostam.

There was once a king of ancient and noble lineage who ruled over a land that had been blessed by God. This land, Barakat, lying on the route of one of the old Silk Roads, had for centuries received the cultural influences of many different worlds. Its geography, too, was diverse: it bordered the sea; then the desert, sometimes bleak with its ancient ruins, sometimes golden and studded with oases, stretched inland for many miles, before meeting the foothills of snow-capped mountains that captured the rain clouds and forced them to deliver their burden in the rich valleys. It was a land of magic and plenty and a rich and diverse heritage.

But it was also a land of tribal rivalries and not infrequent skirmishes. Because the king had the ancient blood of the Quraishi kings in his veins, no one challenged his right to the throne, but many of the tribal chieftains whom he ruled were in constant jealousy over their lands and rights against the others.

One day, the king of this land fell in love with a foreign woman. Promising her that he would never take another wife, he married her and made her his queen. This beloved wife gave him two handsome sons. The king loved them as his own right hand. Crown Prince Zaid and his brother were all that he could wish for in his sons—handsome, noble, brave warriors, and popular with his people. As they attained the age of majority, the sheikh could look forward to his own death without fear for his country, for if anything should happen to the Crown Prince, his brother Aziz would step into his shoes and be equally popular with the people and equally strong among the tribes.

Then one day, tragedy struck the sheikh and his wife.

Both their sons were killed in the same accident. Now his own death became the great enemy to the old man, for with it, he knew, would come certain civil war as the tribal chieftains vied for supremacy.

His beloved wife understood all his fears, but she was by now too old to hope to give him another heir. One day, when all the rituals of mourning were complete, the queen said to her husband, "According to the law, you are entitled to four wives. Take, therefore, my husband, three new wives, that God may bless one of them with a son to inherit your throne."

The sheikh thanked her for releasing him from his promise. A few weeks later, on the same day so that none should afterwards claim supremacy, the sheikh married three beautiful young women, and that night, virile even in his old age, he visited each wife in turn, no one save himself knowing in which order he visited them. To each wife he promised that if she gave him a son, her son would inherit the throne of Barakat.

The sheikh was more virile than he knew. Each of his new wives conceived, and gave birth, nine months later, to a lusty son. And each was jealous for her own son's inheritance. From that moment the sheikh's life became a burden to him, for each of his new young wives had different reasons for believing that her own son should be named the rightful heir to the throne.

The Princess Goldar, whose exotically hooded green eyes she had bequeathed to her son, Omar, based her claim on the fact that she herself was a descendant of the ancient royal family of her own homeland, Parvan.

The Princess Nargis, mother of Rafi and descended from the old Mughal emperors of India, had in addition given birth two days before the other two wives, thus making her son the firstborn.

The Princess Noor, mother of Karim, claimed the inheritance for her son by right of blood—she alone of the wives was an Arab of noble descent, like the sheikh himself. Who but her son to rule the desert tribesmen?

The sheikh hoped that his sons would solve his dilemma for him, that one would prove more princely than the others. But as they grew to manhood, he saw that each of them was, in his own way, worthy of the throne, that each had the nobility the people would look for in their king, and talents that would benefit the kingdom were he to rule.

When his sons were eighteen years old, the sheikh knew that he was facing death. As he lay dying, he saw each of his young wives in turn. To each of them again he promised that her son would inherit. Then he saw his three sons together, and on them he laid his last command. Then, last of all, he saw the wife and companion of his life, with whom he had seen such happiness and such sorrow. To her willing care he committed his young wives and their sons, with the assistance of his vizier Nizam al Mulk, whom he appointed Regent jointly with her.

When he died the old sheikh's will was revealed: the kingdom was to be divided into three principalities. Each of his sons inherited one principality and its palace. In addition, they each inherited one of the ancient Signs of Kingship.

It was the will of their father that they should consult the Grand Vizier Nizam al Mulk for as long as he lived, and appoint another mutual Grand Vizier upon his death, so that none would have partisan advice in the last resort.

Their father's last command had been this: that his sons should never take up arms against each other or any of their descendants, and that his sons and their descendants should always come to each other's aid in times of trouble. The sheikh's dying curse would be upon the head of any who violated this command, and upon his descendants for seven generations.

So the three princes grew to maturity under the eye of the old queen and the vizier, who did their best to prepare the princes for the future. When they reached the age of *twenty-five, they came into their inheritance. Then each prince took his own Sign of Kingship and departed to his own palace and his own kingdom, where they lived in peace and accord with one another, as their father had commanded.*

One

A horseman, his companions lined on either side, his black charger beneath him, galloped across the desert under the morning sun, while the wind scorched his face and lungs, and his horse's tail streamed out behind. His companions, in high spirits with the impromptu race, laughed and called, their voices ringing on the air as they urged their mounts on.

Some distance ahead of them, beyond a harsh rocky outcrop enclosing a few date palms, stood the fallen white stone pillars of an ancient ruin, encircled by the low green roofs of tents. But it was not towards this settlement that they headed. The goal of the race was the rocky outcrop and its sparkling waterfall and pools. The rider on the black broke from the rank with a cry, surged ahead of the others and passed through a narrow defile in the rock walls, one arm and his horse's tail high in the air to signal his triumph.

His companions followed closely, but the gap was torturous and some were obliged to check their mounts as

others passed in. Three who were hot behind were in time
to see their leader halt his snorting mount abruptly and give
a smothered cry. Then they, too, pulled up in amazement.

To see a woman in the desert is not entirely unexpected,
of course. To see a half-naked, perfectly formed beauty of
delicate stature standing under the waterfall of their favourite resting place, her curling black hair streaming down
around her shoulders and back as she raised her face and
arms to the cool torrent, was like something out of the
ancient tales.

Still unconscious of their presence, for no doubt the
sound of their hooves had been smothered by the thunder
of water in her ears, the girl lazily moved out of the stream
of water, opened her eyes, and saw them. Her eyes and
mouth opened wide for a moment of startled stillness as
she stared at the dark, handsome horsemen all around her.

There was silence. Then the girl stepped a little away
from the waterfall on the rock ledge and said gravely, *"Salaam aleikum."*

Her accent was foreign, and so was her cool, haughty
dignity, the faint air of challenge. The leader gazed speech-
lessly. She was lovely as a gazelle, the water drying on her
skin as he watched, leaving it soft and glowing, her mouth
the perfect bow of the ancient paintings that adorned his
palace, her wet hair a wild mane of curls that the paintings
also showed. Her breasts were high and rounded, her hips
slim but very female. Her bathing suit was a soft colour
that matched her lightly browned skin. Her legs were slender and curved, her bare feet sure on the smooth wet rock.

His brain stupidly told him that she was one of the Peri
of the old tales. In a moment she would disappear.

Around him his men flicked him glances and waited for
their lord to speak. Her dark eyes, too, were upon him. Her
eyes had been drawn to him from the first, and she seemed
to realize that he was their leader.

He gazed steadily at her. When the silence stretched too
long he saw alarm kindle behind her gaze, and then, still

speechless, he saw decision there and watched aghast as she turned and agilely began to climb the dangerous rock face beside the falling water. It was not a long way up to that other small pool above. In a moment, just as in the tales of Peris, she had indeed disappeared.

Around him, his men began to talk and exclaim. The leader shook himself as if from a dream. He realized that, from the moment of their entering the place, no more than a minute or two had passed. In so short a space of time, his world had changed.

"What the heck is happening out there?" Gordon asked. Most of the team were already sitting around the long lunch table by the time he arrived, stepping under the long green canvas roof with relief and pulling off the hat that was an absolute necessity for anyone working under the blazing sun.

"Haven't you heard?" squealed Lena, delighted to have someone to pass the news on to, since she herself had been one of the last to hear. "That's the tent of the sultan himself going up."

Gordon blinked, but whether it was from his eyes' difficulty in acclimatizing to the shadow or from astonishment was impossible to say.

"We've all been invited to dinner tonight, the whole team," Ryan, the site director, informed him. "Those are his minions out there preparing for the feast."

Gordon strode to the edge of the canvas shelter and gazed out over the desert to where the circular red-and-blue tent was going up. "It looks the size of a football stadium," he observed mildly. "How many of us does he think there are?"

Gordon was English and it was a point of honour with him never to show excitement. Zara had seen the facade crack only once—when the first clear evidence was found that they really were at the site of ancient Iskandiyar, that all his educated guesswork had paid off at last. This would be the crown of his long career as an archaeologist. They had all stood around cheering and jumping for joy then, and Gordon had joined in. No mere feast laid on by the Prince of East Barakat would evoke such a response in him, though.

"He asked for exact numbers," Zara said now, "but who knows how many of his own court will be in attendance?"

Someone said, "What's the point of it all? Why is he doing it?"

"To welcome us to his country, according to his messenger."

"We've been in his country for three months."

"The wheels of princes grind slowly."

"I suppose it's possible that someone finally gave him the message I sent telling him that we had found the gates that confirm that this is ancient Iskandiyar," said Gordon.

"Maybe he figures it's time to check up on us in case we're about to find treasure."

"He's as rich as a sheikh already," said Warren.

"He *is* a sheikh," Lena pointed out in her scratchy, breathless voice. "He's not married, either," she went on. She was completely unaware of the non sequitur, and when the shout of laughter went up she looked around.

"Why are you all laughing? He really isn't, I heard it on the radio. Don't you remember when that woman was kidnapped by the sheikh of West Barakat awhile ago when that guy stole something from him?" Of course they all remembered, they had talked of nothing else for days. "Then she ended up engaged to him. They said then that his two brothers weren't married."

Lena sighed, making them all laugh again. She blinked at the grinning faces around her and shrugged good-humouredly. "All right, what did I say this time?"

"Nothing, Lena, it's just that you're so obviously hoping that this one will kidnap *you*," Zara told her kindly.

"Oh, am I that obvious? Well, a girl can dream, can't she?"

Zara shuddered involuntarily. She still hadn't told the others about her experience at the wadi. Partly because she knew she would get blamed: they had all been warned that there were bandits in the desert and they should never venture off the dig unaccompanied. But there was more to her reluctance to talk about the incident than that.

She had felt so exposed when the bandit chief—she supposed he must have been that—had stared at her. It was as if her whole being had stopped for a moment while he had entered like a conqueror and taken possession. Even now she wasn't sure what had given her the strength to break out of the prison of his gaze and climb the rock face. Or why he had let her escape.

She had been terrified that when she got to the other side of the outcrop he and his men would be waiting there, and when he was not she had run, slipping and gasping, sobbing with exertion, all the way to the camp, not looking back, but with every cell of her body listening for the sound of hooves.

She knew that Lena was a fool to fantasize about being kidnapped—it must be a dreadful, hellish experience, and if that *had* been the bandit's impulse she was glad he hadn't acted on it. And yet there was a part of her that was sorry to think she would never see him again…sorry that…

"Listen, that reminds me," she said now, still unwilling, but knowing it had to be confessed. "I think I ran into that bandit and his men."

That got their attention. Some of them choked on their coffee, and everyone's eyes were on her. "Where?" two or three demanded at once.

"I went to the wadi early a couple of days ago," she said softly.

"By yourself?" said Gordon. "Zara, that was very unwise."

"Yes, well, I won't do it again. They galloped in while I was standing under the waterfall. I didn't hear a thing. I opened my eyes and there they all were, on horseback, snorting and stamping.''

''The bandits were snorting and stamping?''

They laughed lightly, but this was serious and no one was pretending it wasn't. ''Did they see you? How did you get away?''

Zara swallowed. She was not sure why she was so reluctant to tell them the details. ''I went up over the rocks and ran like hell.''

''If they'd seen you they could have caught up with you, on horseback,'' someone said. ''They must not have seen you.''

Zara said nothing, got up and wandered over to the fridge to get a cold drink, then leaned against it, drinking and staring out over the site, leaving the rest of the team to talk over this latest development.

She was amazingly lucky to be on this dig, which was now certain to make archaeological history. The fourth- and third-century B.C. city called Iskandiyar had been mentioned by several classical authors. Its whereabouts had puzzled modern archaeologists, though, because it was described as being on the banks of the river which now bore the name Sa'adat, Happiness. For more than a century travellers had searched in vain for some sign of it. Such an important city should have left extensive ruins.

Some had even suggested that the classical writers were confused, or inaccurate…but Gordon had never doubted them. Gordon had researched Iskandiyar throughout his career, and one day had stumbled on a much later reference to the fact that, ''in her lifetime Queen Halimah of Barakat built bridges and tunnels and many public buildings. She changed the course of rivers, even the mighty River Sa'adat, when it suited her…''

That was the clue he needed. If the course of the river had been changed eighteen hundred years after the city had been built, then it followed that the city's ruins would no longer be on the banks of the river.

By good luck and good timing, Zara was taking Gordon's classes during the time that he found a possible site in the desert south of the river, and by even better chance she had graduated by the time his funding was in place. And best of all, he had offered her a place on the team.

Until they had uncovered the massive marble lion from the sands of time, there could be certainty only in their hearts. But the classical authors had described Iskandiyar's "Lion Gates," and now it was proven almost beyond doubt. This was a city founded by Alexander the Great on his victorious Eastern march more than two thousand, three hundred years ago. Not long after his conquest here, he would weep because there were no more worlds to conquer.

And now here she was, finding history and making it at the same time. Zara gazed out at the white pillars that shone so harshly in the fierce sun. She wondered sometimes about Alexander's tears on that occasion. Had there been a hollow inside him that he could ignore as long as he kept on the move, kept fighting, kept conquering all he met and saw? Was it a lack in his own life rather than the lack of new worlds that had made him weep?

Zara wasn't thirty-three, the age by which Alexander had conquered the then known world, and although to be associated with such exciting success was a wonderful piece of luck for someone so young, she still had plenty of worlds left to conquer. But sometimes she had the urge to weep, because in unguarded moments her life seemed empty. She didn't understand why. It was as if she had a voice inside telling her she had missed something, had left something out, as though there was something else she should have done or be doing.

She loved her work. She had always loved history, right from the moment she had understood what history was. She enjoyed the mental exercise of trying to understand old ways, the things that had motivated cultures long disappeared. As a child she had been taken on a class field trip to a new archaeological dig on a site in downtown Toronto, and she could still remember her thrilled amazement when she realized that history could be touched, smelt, dug up out of the ground. From that moment she had known what she wanted to do with her life.

Nothing at all stood in her way. She got the marks, she was accepted at the University of Toronto, and Gordon had recognized her commitment and taken her under his wing, as he had several promising students before her, who now had reputations of their own in the field. She couldn't have asked for a better start to her professional career than to work under a man of Gordon's calibre on a find of such importance.

Her personal life was comfortable. She had had an easy, fairly happy childhood, and had come through the teenage years with only a couple of years of tears and slamming doors and impossible parents before things had righted themselves. Zara dated only casually, and kept things light. Of course one day she hoped to fall in love, but she was in no hurry.

And yet...like Alexander, she wanted to weep.

Why? What was missing from her life? What did she want?

For no reason at all, she was suddenly remembering the piercing eyes of the bandit chief as he stared at her on that morning a few days before. There had been another world in his eyes, a world far from her own neat, comfortable existence. That dark, hungry gaze had promised her a passion, a way of living she had never even dreamed of...till now.

For a moment she thought of what it would have meant if he had come after her...swung her up on his horse and ridden away with her. They said he might try to take a hostage, but he had not looked at her like a man who sees a potential hostage. Zara shivered at the memory of how he had looked at her.

She had run harder, faster than she had ever run in her life to escape him. Her heart had never beaten so hard. She closed her eyes, shutting out the glare of the sun on the desert, but the bandit's eyes were still with her.

Two

The preparations at the sheikh's tent went on all afternoon. Helicopters flew in, disgorging lines of people carrying food and supplies, and took them away again; men came and went in Jeeps and on horseback. Except for a moment when it seemed as if the half-erected tent would blow away in a sudden breeze, no shouting was heard, there was no running. Everything was done with an orderly calm and neatness that, as Lena said, made the archaeological team feel "sort of like a low-budget film."

One thing the women were all agreed upon, and that was the necessity of dressing in their best for the feast. By common consent everyone downed tools early to take time to prepare. One of the volunteers produced an iron and asked if she could plug it into the generator lead. The other women fell on this with cries of delight.

"How wonderful! Whatever made you think of it, Jess?"

"I didn't. My mom packed for me. I told her I'd never use it, but she insisted."

"I kiss your mother. Please thank her from all of us in your next letter!"

"I don't have an ironing board, though."

"A towel! All we need is a towel on one of the tables..."

The men went away scratching their heads.

There were lineups for the shower and for the iron, and a lot of excited repartee as people dashed to and fro. Fortunately nearly everyone had something suitable to wear, since everyone had expected to be sampling the city nightlife of the Barakat Emirates some time or other during their stay. But some—the lucky ones—had what Gordon called "the full monty." Including Gordon himself, who stunned everyone when he appeared just before time in white tie and tails and polished shoes.

"Can't let the side down," he said by way of explanation when the others fell back in amazement at this vision of British Establishment eccentricity.

"Gee, Gordon," Lena said in stunned tones, "it's just like one of those films—you wearing all that in the desert and all."

Blonde Lena herself got the prize for feminine magnificence in a low-cut, blush pink dress under a matching gauzy pink georgette coat embroidered in the Eastern fashion with lots of silver thread.

But it was Zara who really stopped them in their tracks. Small and slender, wearing a beautifully simple, high-necked, long-sleeved white dress in heavy raw silk that hung straight and smooth to her bare brown feet in delicate gold sandals, her curling cloak of hair spilling over her shoulders and down her back, one gold bangle at her wrist, she was a vision. Lena eyed her with mock dismay.

"I dunno, you kinda make me feel overdone," she observed plaintively. But a chorus of voices assured her that many men preferred the obvious, and large numbers of those who did were Oriental potentates.

"And me," said one male voice. Greg moved to her side and mock-ferociously put an arm around her, leering down into her cleavage. "Any Oriental potentate is going to have to get past me first."

"That'll take about a minute," another man observed.

Lena giggled and rolled her eyes. "Oh, Greg, as if I'd look at you if the prince wanted me!"

"Right, are we all here?" said Gordon's dry voice above the nervous, excited banter. "Before we start, may I just remind you all that we will very likely be sitting on cushions on the floor, and that it is considered rude in this part of the world to direct the soles of your feet at anyone. So don't think you can lie stretched out with your ankles crossed and feet pointing towards the prince. You sit with your feet tucked under you, one way or another. In addition—" He gave them several more pointers and then consulted his watch and said, "Right. Time we were off."

And in a column of twos and threes they left the dining enclosure and began to move across the sand in the direction of what they were still laughingly calling the sultan's tent.

They had barely set out when they saw lights, and a moment later they were greeted by a party of servants with flaming torches and a man dressed in peacock blue magnificence who bowed and introduced himself as Arif ur-Rashid, Cup Companion to the Prince.

"Very flattering," Gordon muttered into Zara's ear. "By tradition the further the king or his emissary comes to meet his guests, the higher the honour. We've been met effectively at our own doorstep. Very nice indeed. I think we can look forward to a substantial feast. Pearls in the bottom of our wine goblets and told to keep them sort of thing."

Zara gurgled into laughter. She was one of the few who recognized when Gordon was joking, and his eyes glinted approvingly down at her.

But it wasn't quite so much of a joke as he had imagined. All the archaeological team gasped with awe when they passed through the doors into the tent.

It was like entering Aladdin's cave. Everything glowed

with richness and warmth. The colours were deep and luxurious—emerald, ruby, sapphire, turquoise. Every inch of
walls, floor and ceiling was hung and draped with carpets,
tapestries, or beautifully dyed cloth, and the furniture—of
walnut, mahogany and other unknown, fabulously grained
woods—had such a deep polish it seemed as if it would
shine "even if no fire touched it."

All the light came from naked flame, or flame under
delicately painted or cut crystal globes that sent light shim-
mering around the room like a thousand flung diamonds.
And all around them were handsome men in exotic dress
introducing themselves as the Cup Companions of the
prince. The team felt as if they had stepped back centuries
in time, straight into the pages of the *Arabian Nights*.

One of the Companions had visited the dig earlier in the
afternoon, and had been introduced to every member of the
team by Gordon, and now they were all greeted by name.
For several minutes they made conversation.

Then the heavy sound of a helicopter was heard close
by. There was an expectant pause, during which the team
found it impossible to chat normally. All of them were
surreptitiously watching the entrance. Suddenly a group of
men erupted into the room, talking and laughing, and bringing a vital and very appealing energy with them. As one
man, the Companions in the room turned and bowed.

The new arrivals were all just as exotically and colour-
fully dressed as the Companions, and the brilliance of the
prince himself was breathtakingly unmistakable.

His long, high-necked jacket was cream silk and seemed
to be studded with pinpoints of green light from elbow to
wrist and around the collar. His flowing Eastern trousers
were deep green. Diagonally across his breast he wore a
cloth-of-gold sash, and a double rope of absolutely magnificent pearls at least a yard long was looped and draped
over his chest, and fixed at one shoulder with a ruby the
size of an egg. He had a lustrous black moustache and
thick, waving black hair, which, like the heads of all his

Companions, was bare. His fingers were clustered with a king's ransom in gold and stones.

He put up one arrogant hand in a gesture that in any other man would look, Zara thought, ridiculously theatrical, but in him seemed perfectly natural and engaging. Smiling broadly, he recited something in Arabic, and then said in English, "It is very kind of you all to come to my poor table. May so propitious an occasion be blessed."

The efforts of the team to think of some suitable response would have made Zara laugh if she hadn't been similarly dumbstruck herself.

Prince Rafi recognized Gordon in the throng and strode to his side to greet the director, where Arif joined him. The prince chatted briefly to Gordon and then Arif introduced Maeve, then followed the prince slowly through the room, introducing him to each member of the team. The prince tilted his head solicitously to each and shook their hands, exchanging a few words before moving on.

He made his way around the room and at last appeared at Zara's side. Now she was aware of two things not quite so obvious from a distance—a heady yet elusive scent of sandalwood or myrrh or something similar, and the powerful physical aura of the man. He was not tall, but he exuded power.

"Miss Zara Blake, Your Highness," said Arif, and a well-shaped, graceful hand was extended to her. Aware that she was blushing, Zara flicked her eyes to his face as she put her hand into his. "Miss Blake, His Serene Highness Sayed Hajji Rafi Jehangir ibn Daud ibn Hassan al Quraishi."

The name rolled off his tongue like poetry.

"Miss Blake, it is a very great pleasure," said the prince in a tiger's fur voice, with such emphasis she almost believed him.

"How do you do, Your Highness," Zara murmured, finding that, whatever her democratic principles, her head seemed to bow of its own accord. Dimly she supposed that was the definition of true royalty—when you couldn't help bowing.

"I hope your stay in my country will be long and fruitful," he said.

Zara looked up again, but found that she could not meet his dark eyes for long. She blushed even more warmly, though she had hardly blushed in her life. "Your Highness is very kind," she murmured.

She expected him to move on then—he had only exchanged a few words with each of the others—but to her surprise he asked, "Your name is Zara?" He pronounced it with a little explosion of air on the first vowel. *Zahra.*

"Yes."

"This is a very beautiful name. In my language it means both *flower* and *splendour, beauty.*" Without saying it, he managed to imply that she was well named.

"Ah…oh."

"Are your parents perhaps Arabic speakers?"

"No…my father's background is French and my mother—" she shrugged and tried to smile "—just plain Canadian. Sort of mixed."

Zara was amazed to find herself so stumbling and confused. It was not at all like her, and she was furious with herself. He was a prince only by the luck of birth, and his compliments were no more significant than anyone else's! There was no reason to start blushing like a fifteen-year-old. A glance around the room showed her that the others had noticed his interest. Passionately she wished he would move on to the next team member.

He did not. She looked at him again in time to intercept the tiniest flick of his long black lashes to Arif ur-Rashid.

The Companion nodded, raised his mellifluous voice slightly for attention, and said, "Here in Barakat, ladies and gentlemen, we do not follow the Western custom of preliminary drinks and hors d'oeuvres while standing. You are invited now to sit at the prince's table."

The wall behind Zara suddenly opened, and only then

did she notice the big wooden arch she had been standing in front of, revealed as a doorway as servants lifted the heavy draperies that had closed it.

Prince Rafi lifted his arm. "Allow me to escort you, Zara."

At the sound of her name on his lips, Zara stiffened a little. Okay, this had gone far enough, and it was going to stop right here, before she found herself ensconced in the harem.

"Thank you, Rafi," she said coolly, and put her hand on his arm.

He smiled into her eyes and drooped his eyelids with pleasure, tilting his head in acknowledgement. Zara gasped a little. She was a fool to play games in so different a culture. She had no idea what message she had just sent him. For all she knew she had already said yes to a post-prandial romp.

And, she recollected somewhat belatedly, she had more than herself to think of. The whole future of the dig was under this man's sole sway. He could wave one graceful, masculine hand and the desert would be clear of them to-morrow.

The archaeological team filed after them through the arched doorway and into the dining room, where they stopped amazed, cries of astonishment soft on their lips, and feeling just a little, Zara thought, like barbarians seeing civilisation for the first time. Among them, the Companions moved with polished grace, inviting them individually to sit.

Prince Rafi led her all the length of the room while Zara gazed in unaffected delight at the spectacle before them. Dozens—hundreds!—of multicoloured silk and tapestry cushions lay massed around the long, low rectangular table that stood about six inches off the ground. It shone with cut crystal and painted porcelain, silver and old gold. Down the centre of the table and all around the walls could be seen the flicker of numerous flames under the most artistically painted glass globes. Against one wall there was a large fountain—she couldn't believe it, but it was a real marble fountain, and the sound of the softly splashing water was better than music. All along the opposite wall, panels had been rolled up to allow the gentle night breeze to cool them, and the moon and the stars and the desert to form part of the decor. Zara had never seen anything to equal it in her life.

"It's very beautiful," she said quietly, and Prince Rafi smiled.

"I am very happy to please you, Zara." He led her to the farther end of the table. The smell of cooking food rose deliciously on the air.

Prince Rafi stopped and guided her to a place. He stood beside her, and with a curious sinking elation she understood that she had been chosen to sit beside him during the meal. A Companion was on his other side, and next to the Companion was Gordon. All around, the others were finding their places, and in a moment it became clear that every second or third place was taken by one of the Cup Companions.

Prince Rafi raised his arms and gestured them to sit. Zara settled herself among the most comfortable cushions she had ever sat on in her life, and tucked her feet neatly beside her. She turned to find that Arif ur-Rashid was on her other side.

Music started playing. Several musicians with stringed and other instruments—some of which she had never seen before—had come in and settled in a corner and were playing a soft accompaniment to the coming meal.

Arif clapped his hands, and a small army of white-clad boys and girls appeared, each boy carrying a pitcher, each girl a basin, all in silver chased with gold. They approached the table and knelt by the diners. One girl knelt between Prince Rafi and Zara, and, balancing the basin on her knee, offered the prince a bar of soap. He spoke a few gentle words, and she blushed and turned to Zara, offering her the bar. Grateful that Gordon had warned them of the ritual, she took the offered bar and washed her hands lightly under the flow of water that the boy produced from the pitcher.

When Zara had finished, the girl reached to take the soap from her, but her hand fell back as Prince Rafi's own hand stretched across the basin. Her heart beating hard with unaccustomed confusion, Zara slipped the perfumed soap into his hand. His dark hand closed firmly on the slender white bar, and Zara's mouth opened, gasping for more oxygen than seemed to be available. She watched transfixed as he stroked the bar of soap into a lather between his hands, then, as if without volition, felt her gaze drawn upwards to his face.

He was watching her, a half smile in his dark eyes. Slowly, lazily, he set the soap in the basin and held his hands under the stream the boy carefully poured. The scent of rosewater mingled with the other subtle scents assailing her nostrils.

"The towel is offered you, Miss Blake," said the prince, and she blinked and smiled at the worried girl who was holding the soft oblong of fabric up for her.

"Thank you," she said. She dried her hands and watched as the prince did the same. Then the boy and girl moved away to join the phalanx of water bearers, who all bowed and then filed neatly out of the room.

Almost immediately another group of servants filed in, bringing with them this time the welcome, delicious odour of food. Within the next few minutes a feast appeared. Some dishes were placed on the table, some were carried around and offered to the guests. The beautiful silver and gold goblets were filled with water and wine and exotic juices.

After the bustle had died down, Prince Rafi lifted his gold cup. "I extend to all members of the archaeological team my congratulations on the important historical site which you have discovered and will no doubt in the years to come excavate, to enrich the knowledge of my country's

and the world's ancient history. In particular, I commend
Mr. Gordon Rhett, whom I know well from those occasions
when he visited and wrote to me in his enthusiasm for this
project.''

He turned and saluted Gordon with his glass, and everybody drank.

''But now is not the time for speeches. The pleasures of
the mind are offered when the pleasures of the flesh have
been satisfied.'' He invited them all to eat and drink, but
Zara could hardly take in the words. When he said those
words, ''the pleasures of the flesh,'' it was as if his body
sparked with electricity so strong she received a shock from
it. She was covered in gooseflesh.

She thought, *I'm helpless already. If he really does want
me, I won't be able to refuse.*

Three

———

It became clearer and clearer as the evening wore on that Prince Rafi had eyes only for Zara. Whether he was speaking to the whole room, or to an individual, or listening or silent, there was a kind of glow around the two, apparent to almost everyone in the room. Several times, as if hardly realizing it, the prince would break off what he was saying to lean over and encourage Zara to try the most delicious tidbit on the platter that was being offered, or to signal the cupbearers to refill her glass, or to ask her with an intimate smile whether she liked some flavour.

When the whole roast sheep came in, he regaled them all with the story of the time his father had, according to custom, made the grand gesture of giving one of the sheep's eyes to his most honoured guest—the British Ambassador. He mimicked the British Ambassador's false expressions of gratitude.

He was a magical storyteller, with the knack of making

people laugh. "Did he have to eat it in front of everyone?" Zara asked.

Prince Rafi turned lazily approving eyes upon her, which shocked her system as if with an unexpected touch. "My stepmother, my father's first and most beloved wife, was then a new bride. She was sitting on the other side of the Ambassador. Just after the sheep's eye was served to him, my stepmother had the misfortune to knock over her water glass. The ambassador certainly put something into his mouth and ate it with great enjoyment. But it was rumoured that my stepmother afterwards berated my father and made him swear never again to offer sheep's eyes to a foreign guest."

They were all laughing. Rafi watched in admiration how Zara's neck arched, her eyes brimming over with mischief and merriment, her black lustrous curls falling just so with the tilt of her elegant head.

"My stepmother was a foreigner herself," he said then. "She understood the ways of foreigners, and she gave my father much good advice. She was of great assistance to him in his rule. He always said so." He paused. "They were much in love, all their lives."

He said this gazing right at Zara. The laughter died in her, and heat crept visibly up her cheeks. She was beginning to be a little angry now. Making eyes at her was one thing. This was getting ridiculous. She was starting to feel like an idiot.

She returned his look coolly. "It didn't stop him taking other wives, though, did it? She was not, after all, your own mother."

Instead of chilling him, this comment had the effect of making his eyes spark with interest, as if she had betrayed jealousy and he counted that a point in his favour. "Ah, you do not know my father's tragic story!" Rafi exclaimed. He looked around at the musicians. "Where is Motreb? Ask him to come forth."

A man in curious dress entered carrying yet another unfamiliar stringed instrument not unlike a banjo. "Motreb, I ask you to sing for my friends the song of my father's love," cried Prince Rafi.

He leaned to Haroun on his left and murmured a word in his ear, and when the singer-storyteller settled himself to sing the song of the great king who fell in love with a bewitching foreigner, the Companion got up and stood beside him. Between the plaintive lines, Motreb paused, playing his instrument, while Haroun translated the story of King Daud.

"'And will you take no wife but me? You cannot swear to this, quoth she.'"

Zara, who had never heard the story, was entranced, both by the tale itself and by the haunting ululating melody of the singer's voice.

"'I will. I swear. No wife but thee...'"

Then she heard the story of how King Daud had married the stranger and to the great joy of his people, had made her his queen. And how thirty years of happy marriage and two sons followed, giving no warning before disaster struck in the shape of a fatal air crash. The king and queen mourned long.

"'We have lost our beloved sons, my husband. And though with all my heart I would give you more, I am old...your promise, too, made in the sweet blossom of youth, is old. I say it is no more. It has died with our sons. Take therefore, my husband, three young wives, and get a son for your kingdom, that this land may remain what men call Blessed.'"

Zara's eyes burned as the tragic voice sobbed out the story. Somewhere on her right she heard a sniff, Lena probably, which made her own control slip. She dropped her head, surreptitiously pulling a tissue out of her bag with one hand, and dabbed her eyes.

Her free hand was taken in a firm but gentle hold, and her eyes flew to Prince Rafi. He drew her hand up, gave her a long, slow, dark and sexy look, and kissed her knuckles once, twice. Not a simple pressure of the mouth, either, but a dragging pressure from parted lips, his eyes half closed, as if he wanted to eat her. Her body seemed to melt in spite of all her determination to be unaffected. Her heart had been knocked from its moorings and lay kicking helplessly in her breast.

After that, she had trouble swallowing. Never had she experienced so public or so determined a seduction. When the song was over, Prince Rafi himself poured wine into a silver goblet for the singer, who drained it to find a large pearl at the bottom as his reward. He bowed and retired, and there was a pause in the entertainments and the buzz of conversation arose.

The song was followed by stories from one or two Companions, then by gymnastic young performers, then by a very artful belly dancer in the most bewitching costume Zara had ever seen, then by another song. All the artists seemed to be paid with jewels or gold, in scenes straight from the *Arabian Nights*.

Meanwhile, the food came in a never-ending supply. And so did the approving looks from Prince Rafi's dark eyes. Zara's heart seemed to kick into a new, higher, faster rhythm with each look.

He was staggeringly charismatic—handsome, virile, with a smile women probably jumped off cliffs for. But he was also a desert chieftain, however rich, and her own inner response to his admiration frightened her. A girl should have some resistance if she was going to be propositioned, and Zara felt she had no more resistance than a kitten.

When the last empty tray had been carried away, small silver salvers laden with soft Turkish delight in powdered sugar began to make the rounds, and there seemed to be general movement among the guests, led by the Companions. But when Zara tried to get up, Prince Rafi's firm hand was on her arm. And she was too much of a coward to resist the implied command.

After a few moments, Prince Rafi made a signal to the

Companion named Ayman, who had changed his seat and was now lounging on the cushions beside Lena, to the obvious displeasure of Arif. With a nod to his prince and then to Lena, the Companion got to his feet and left the room.

"It was a tradition among my forebears to give robes of honour to those who had performed some signal service," Prince Rafi began. "Since each of you contributes to the overall achievement of proving not only that the great Iskandar, whom you call Alexander, visited this land, but also uncovering the city that he himself founded, it is my pleasure to reward each of you with the traditional robe of honour. Even so would Alexander have been presented with a robe by my own predecessor."

At that moment, Ayman returned, leading a train of the boys and girls who had been the water bearers at the start of the evening. Each youth was the bearer this time of a neat cube of folded cloth, all of different colours, in stripes or swirls or solids, glittering with gold and silver threads. Each knelt at the side of one member of the team and offered the robe.

There were loud squeals of surprised and appreciative delight from all the women, but the men, too, were clearly very pleased. People began jumping to their feet to unfold the robes and try them on.

A pretty girl, gazing in deep admiration at Zara, knelt beside her, her arms full of glittering cloth. Zara thanked her. The child flicked a glance at Prince Rafi, who nodded approvingly. To Zara's surprise, the girl smiled affectionately at the prince, who winked at her, before bowing and departing.

"Who are these servant children?" Zara asked.

Prince Rafi laughed. "They are not servants! They are young courtiers. They are the younger sisters and brothers of my Companions, or my own cousins...all are educated at the palace. As well as academic subjects and languages, they learn the rules of hospitality."

All around, people were on their feet, trying on and admiring their robes. "Oh, my!" Zara exclaimed breathlessly, as she began to examine her own gift. It seemed to be made of spun gold, and embroidered with fabulous designs in red and green. She had never seen anything so rich and lustrous outside of a medieval painting. "But it's *beautiful!*" she whispered helplessly. "I can't possibly…"

Not far away, Gordon was standing up to model his own very rich robe. Hearing her cry, he glanced down and gave her an admonitory look, which she interpreted as meaning that it would be a grave insult to refuse a robe of honour. If she insulted the prince, the dig might be history. She knew they were hoping to convince the prince to contribute the funding they would need to keep it going beyond this season.

"It's very beautiful," she murmured, drawing her feet under her haunches and struggling to stand gracefully amid the cushions. But her foot was on the hem of her dress and before she knew what was happening she had fallen straight onto Prince Rafi.

His arms quickly caught her, and his eyes closed as her long black hair spilled over him. The robe of honour tumbled from Zara's hands and was splayed out around them, glittering in the lamp flame like something magical, a thing of inestimable value.

Prince Rafi inhaled, his eyes closing, and murmured in her ear, "The perfume of your hair would drive a man mad. I have dreamed of you, waking and sleeping."

As a tableau it ranked with the most beautiful miniature paintings in the prince's own extensive collection. Even the Companions were not proof against it. Everyone in the room was frozen in some posture, half with their arms in their robes. All eyes were on them. If she were not so covered with embarrassment, she could have laughed at the picture of so many startled, curious, gawking faces.

But it was her own reaction that was the danger. Zara felt molten, like the golden robe, electrified by the man's touch, his whispered words.

"I—I'm so sorry," she stammered, struggling from his grasp to her feet. "I don't know what made me so clumsy."

"Do you not?" he smiled. He solicitously helped her to gain her feet.

"Ah...well..." She hardly knew what she was saying. Trying for calm, for the ordinary—so far as anything in this remarkable evening could be called ordinary—Zara lifted the robe and put it on.

It was breathtakingly beautiful, utterly rich and luxurious. It fanned out at the back in a broad curving sweep to the floor, while in front it was cut shorter, the hem just skimming her toes. "Thank you," she whispered.

Trying to give her breathing room, Gordon sat down and said to Prince Rafi, "I think I should tell you that one of our team saw a group of mounted bandits the other morning. There seemed to be quite a number of them, and I'm afraid our security may not be sufficient."

Prince Rafi's head straightened with surprise. "Bandits!" he exclaimed. "So near! We do not often see Jalal on our side of the river. His headquarters is in my brother's land. Where, exactly, were they seen?"

"At the wadi. Members of the team go there to relax away from the heat whenever they get a chance. Everyone has been warned not to go off the site alone, but I'm afraid the waterfall there is very tempting."

"At the waterfall?" Rafi repeated, in a different voice. He turned his head towards Zara, who had sat down to listen. "When, and how many?"

Zara smiled. "It was three days ago. I didn't stop to count their numbers. I just took one look and ran! But I think there were ten or twelve, anyway. All on the most magnificent horses."

He was watching her intently. "Were you frightened?"

"Terrified," she agreed without emphasis.

"Their captain—did you see him?"

"I think so," Zara told him, repressing a shiver at the memory of the bandit chief's gaze and her own reaction to it. Not much different from the response Prince Rafi raised in her. Maybe she had a weakness. "There certainly was one man with an air of command."

"And he—did he see you?"

That passionate black gaze rose up in her mind's eye, and, pressing her lips together, Zara only nodded.

"But you were not taken? Twelve men and you escaped?"

"I don't think he—they tried. I am sure if they had ridden out of the enclosure and around—well, on horseback they could have caught up with me before I got back to the tents." Her mouth was dry, she didn't know why. Something she had noticed but which hadn't filtered through to her conscious mind was making her uneasy.

"Then he is a fool," said Prince Rafi. "When a man sees what he wants, should he not take pains to achieve it instantly?"

Zara smiled. "Maybe he didn't see what he wanted," she said, and shivered, knowing it was a lie. The bandit chief had wanted her. There must be something about her that appealed to the Arab temperament, too.

A marriage made in heaven, then, she told herself dryly.

"What man would not have wanted you, so beautiful under the fall of water, your limbs bare and your skin so silken? He must have been jealous even of the eyes of his companions for the fact that they also saw the vision. If he did not pursue you across the sand and catch you up on his horse then, it can only be because he had other plans to obtain you. Did not King Khosrow fall madly in love with Shirin when he caught sight of her bathing? And he stopped at nothing to gain her."

It was the naked passion in his eyes, more than anything else, that told her the truth. He had been veiling it from her all evening, letting her see only a portion of what was there. But now she saw again the black flame of complete and determined need burn up behind his gaze.

Her hand snapping to her open mouth, Zara gasped, an

electric sound that caused conversation everywhere to stop. Her hand slowly lowered, while her eyes gazed helplessly into his. Take away the white keffiyeh that had enwrapped the bandit's head and chin…

"A man would do all in his power," Prince Rafi promised her softly.

"It was you!" she whispered.

His black eyes fixed hers, letting her read the truth. That was the reason, then, for the prince's sudden interest in the team, for this dinner…she saw it all. That was why he had singled her out.

His Serene Highness Sayed Hajji Rafi Jehangir ibn Daud ibn Hassan al Quraishi was the man at the wadi she had thought the bandit chief.

Four

Zara succeeded in tearing her eyes away from the prince's at last, and glanced up to see that the gaze of every member of the archaeological team was rivetted on her. The Companions, more socially skilled, pretended not to notice, and were making light conversation to their inattentive neighbours.

She really couldn't think. She needed air, and solitude.

"Excuse me," she said. Struggling to her feet again, the coat billowing and glowing behind her, Zara walked down the length of the room, past little clusters of people who tried to cover their fascination with chatter but could not help following her with their eyes.

Outside, the full moon glowed on the broad desert, its sweeping dunes, the tents of the archaeological team in the distance, and closer, the outcrop where the tall palms that surrounded the pool and waterfall were just visible above the rocks.

Pressing her hands to her hot cheeks, the robe billowing

behind her, Zara moved towards it. There was a narrow defile in the rocks from this direction, dark now with moonshadow, but she knew her way through. Soon she was inside, listening to the rushing sound of the falling water.

It was Gordon's theory that this was the original course of the river, before Queen Halimah, in one of her public projects, had diverted it, and that an underground stream remained as testimony, forced to the surface here by some geological fault, to form the delicious waterfall and its pools before disappearing underground again.

She was walking where Alexander the Great had probably once walked. Zara sank down on the rocks by the pool and dipped one hand in, leaning over to press the cool water to her cheeks.

The moon was strong, casting black shadows under the walls of rock, but she sat in full moonlight, and it glistened on the water, on her hair, and on her golden robe.

It was two thousand, three hundred and thirty years since Alexander had come here with his armies, but humankind had not changed very much. Men were still consumed by jealousies and passions…and sex was still like this river…try to divert it, and its power went underground, to force its way up at any weak spot…

She did not know what to do about Prince Rafi. That there was a powerful attraction between them she couldn't, wouldn't try to deny. She had felt it for him when she thought him a bandit, and finding him a king had certainly not lessened its force.

But she was a stranger in a strange land, a woman desired by a king. She had no idea what dangers awaited her if she gave in to what she felt, what he wanted. She spoke only a little of the language, knew not nearly enough about the country and its culture. Her knowledge of the area was all of the distant past, and she wasn't sure that the autocratic powers and ways of the ancient kings whose names she knew had altogether passed into history.

Suppose she gave in to him, for one night, or one week,

or…what would it mean, in the end? Did kings let women go after they had loved them, or did they guard them jealously in their harems, not wanting them, but not willing that any other man should ever have the power of being compared with the king as a lover?

Ridiculous. She was sure that was ridiculous. But what was not ridiculous was the fear she felt. The thought of letting him make love to her frightened her. No man had ever made her so nervous.

She heard a clinking sound, and something that sounded like a horse blowing. In sudden alarm, Zara lifted her head.

She was beautiful, a white dress and a flowing golden robe, and her black curling hair another robe over her shoulders and back, like the descriptions by the poets. Her face a painting, the eyebrows darkly curving, the mouth a perfect bow. The mountain tribes had their tales of the Peri, the race of Other, whose tiny beautiful women enticed men and disappeared, but this was the desert. Behind her the moon shimmered on the rustling water.

This was the one. There could not be another.

"Who's there?" Zara called, trying to keep any sign of nerves from her voice, realizing she had been a fool to come wandering out here on her own. "Who is it?"

Suddenly the place seemed eerie, full of danger. Zara shivered and got to her feet. What a fool she was! What if Prince Rafi followed her out here? What if he had construed her movements as an invitation?

She heard a footfall. The waterfall disguised everything, but she thought it came from the passage. It was Prince Rafi. She knew it, and panic filled her blood with the urgent command to flee. She ran light as wind towards the sheltering rocks. Damn the moonlight! It caught in the glittering robe and would betray her whereabouts even in the darkest shadows.

Zara turned her head this way and that, peering through the gloom, trying to remember the layout of the place. There was a niche somewhere, a place to hide, but the shadows were very black. There was no time to think. She flung herself into the unknown.

Then she shrieked as the black horse reared up in front of her. Out of the shadows a body bent down and dark hands reached for her. The prince! *My God, is he mad?* she thought, in the moment before the strong hands grasped her, the powerful arms lifted her, and she felt the horse beneath her thighs and her face was smothered against his chest.

She clung to him for safety, there was nothing else to do. He had already spurred the horse to a wild gallop, and to fall now might kill her. Her heart pounded deafeningly in her ears. In the tiny part of her mind that remained cool, she had time to think, *I didn't scream. I suppose that counts as an invitation in this part of the world.*

She couldn't scream now—she was pressed into his chest, almost smothered. She smelled the odour of male sweat and desert and horse in the all-encompassing burnous he was wearing over his clothes, and the hairs lifted primitively on the back of her neck.

The smell was not right. He had been sandalwood and myrrh, and another scent, all his own, that was missing now.

In the same moment she heard a curse resonate in the chest under her cheek, and the horse veered wildly and half reared, throwing her harder against him. For a moment, one arm loosed her and he wrestled with the reins, and Zara lifted her head and saw a man flung to the ground by the horse's powerful forequarters as they rode past.

In the moonlight the colour of his coat seemed purple, but he was impossible to mistake. Prince Rafi leapt to his feet and gave chase as she watched, but the horseman had goaded his horse into a violent gallop and in seconds he was left far behind.

She screamed then, loud and long, but it was too late. All around her stretched the glow of moonlight on the wide, bleak, empty desert. Fear was nearly overwhelming. She gasped and choked, but before she could scream again the strong hand came up and pressed her face into the stifling folds of the burnous.

She was afraid of falling off the horse as it made its headlong plunge down a cliff of sand, but the suffocating hold was too firm. The sickness of terror was in her throat and she wondered which would be worse—what the bandit had in mind for her, or being crippled or killed under the sharp hooves.

She must get calm. She gained nothing by thinking of what lay ahead. She had to plan. She had already missed a crucial opportunity. If she had not believed it was Prince Rafi on the horse, she might have…but it was no use thinking of that, either. She should think of escape now.

"If you struggle I will tie you over the saddle," the man grunted as she stirred. "If you scream I will knock you on the head." Shivers of terror chased up and down her spine at the threat in his voice. He sounded like a man who said what he meant, who would stop at nothing.

"I can't breathe!" she cried, and he must have some humanity, she thought, because he let her turn her face into the air.

He kept one hand over her mouth, her head pressed back against him. Zara impatiently forced her stupid mind to think. There must be something she could do! They would follow her. Prince Rafi, Gordon—they were sure to chase the bandit. They might already be in the helicopter. And there were the Land Rovers, too.

He had thought of the same thing, she realized, for after a time she could not measure they left the sand and entered an area of stony ground they had been galloping at an angle to for some time, and here he turned the horse so sharply that it was almost facing back on its own path. He had ridden away from the camp towards the east, but now she thought they were headed west north west. How long would it take the searchers to give up on the easterly direction and search other possibilities?

Far to the left now on the clear desert air they heard the sound of the helicopter beating the air. Her head was pressed firmly back against the bandit's chest, but she could just see the light in the distance that told her the helicopter had a searchlight. If only she could leave some sign, some signal of the way they had gone! Something that would shine in the searchlight…her sandals were gold.

She still had both her sandals on. It seemed impossible, after all that had happened. There was a little strap between each toe, fanning out to a lacy pattern over her instep. She had never realized before how firmly they held.

Slowly, trying not to think of what she was doing lest the bandit pick up the thought, Zara worked one sandal off her foot and kicked it free. She didn't look back, didn't try to see how it had fallen. It might be days before it was found, if ever. A few miles later she let the second sandal drop.

The helicopter was going the wrong way, carefully following the horse's first easterly direction. The sound grew faint. Her captor's firm hold on her slackened. "They will not hear you now, if you scream," he told her. But the horse's pace continued.

Her hip felt bruised and she shifted to a more comfortable position. The golden robe was billowing in the wind. She pulled at it, amazed to find that she was still wearing that, too. "Where are you taking me?" she asked. Her throat was hoarse.

"To my camp."

"Isn't your camp on the other side of the river?"

He glanced down at her, the moonlight full on his face, and did not answer. She caught her breath on a gasp.

"You look like Prince Rafi!" she whispered.

The man laughed, flinging his head back. "Do I so?"

Fear chased up and down her spine. "Who are you?"

"Have not you been told tales of me? I am Jalal the Bandit, grandson of the great Selim."

"Who—" Zara began, but he interrupted her.

"Do not waste your breath with asking questions. I will answer nothing and we have a long, hard way to go."

He hadn't been exaggerating. Zara had lost track of time. She had rarely been on a horse for longer than an hour, and she was sitting sidesaddle, one hip thrust higher than the other in a posture that became increasingly uncomfortable as the time passed. She was glad when numbness set in, but even that was painful.

"I must blindfold you now."

She surfaced from the daze she had sunk into, and wondered how long they had been riding. The horse was covered in lather, and obviously miserable, but doing his best for his master.

Jalal lifted an arm and pulled the large keffiyeh from his head. "Wrap this around your head and eyes."

They must be near some landmark that she would be able to identify. She prayed that this meant that he intended to keep her alive—for otherwise why bother about what she saw?—and sobbed once with the relief of a fear she hadn't been letting herself feel.

She cast one last glance around her, trying to memorize the scene, imprint it on her mind, as she reached to take the cloth and wrap her face in it. Ahead there was a mound of rock, made huge with shadow. She thought she heard the sound of running water in the distance, but the desert was full of moonshadows that made it hard to distinguish features.

A buffet of wind caught them then, and her golden robe suddenly snapped and billowed out behind her.... Zara thought, *It's the one certain marker I could leave*—if she could drop it without his noticing. If they found it, Prince Rafi would recognize it, she was certain. He would know that she had passed this way...*if anyone, nomad or trader, ever passes this way,* she told herself ruthlessly. *And if the wind hasn't buried it, and if the nomad takes it to his prince…* but she had to try *something.* If she gave up hope now she was lost.

Under cover of wrapping her head, Zara released one arm from the beautiful robe. Now it was held on only by one arm. She finished wrapping the scarf around her eyes. Then blindly, inch by inch, working by touch alone, she drew the robe into a bundle in her lap.

The horse, very tired now, struggled on for minutes while she nearly suffocated with fear behind the constricting cloth. At last it was reined to a very slow walk. Zara tensed for action. She sensed an echo, their approach to something large. They were about to enter some place. Pulling her arm from the robe, she screamed and began to struggle.

She was no match for the bandit's strength, and her rebellion lasted hardly more than a second. But the robe was now loose in her hands. "Bend down, it is low," he ordered curtly, pushing her flat against the horse's neck and bending over her. This was her last chance. Lying over the horse's neck, Zara dragged the crushed robe from under her and flung it away. A moment later the sounds told her that they were entering something like a cave.

"Cover your face," he ordered again.

Behind them, the golden cloth glittered for a moment in the moonlight as it fell to the desert floor.

Rafi ran all the way to the helicopter and pulled futilely at the door before he realized that Ammar had locked it. Precautions against Jalal, he reflected grimly, but this would give the bandit a head start he would probably never lose. Rafi ran back towards the tent, calling for the Companions. But the party was noisy, drowning his cry as it had drowned the sound of the horse and Zara's scream.

By the time he had reached the tent again, he knew too much time had passed. The bandit could be heading anywhere, and in darkness his trail would not be easy to follow.

At last Rafi was close enough for his cries to be heard, and the party was silenced. There were shouts, and the Companions came spilling out of the tent on the alert. All the archaeological team followed, calling questions.

Rafi curbed his impatience to be gone, told them what had occurred, and gave orders for some to take the land vehicles in a search that would be virtually useless. Even if they could find the trail, the land vehicles would not be able to follow everywhere a horse led.

"He galloped east till he was out of sight," he said. "But he is not a fool. He might be headed anywhere." Seconds later he set off running across the sand back towards the helicopter, with Arif and Ammar silently pacing him.

"What a fool to have set no guard tonight!" he berated himself as they flung themselves into the cockpit and Ammar started the rotors slowly beating.

"Shall we go to his camp, or follow his trail?" demanded Arif as they lifted off.

"Follow his trail," said Rafi briefly, straining to see against the deep moonshadows on the desert.

"His camp is still on the other side of the river, is it not?" Ammar said, as he flicked on the landing light. All three peered out, but this was not a military helicopter and it was not a powerful searchlight. "He can only get across if he goes to the bridge. Why not meet him there, Lord?"

"We do not know that he means to take her to his camp. A man who has plotted to take a hostage for so long may have chosen another place to keep them," said Rafi, his jaw clenched. "Radio Haroun to drive to the bridge." He did not want to think of what conditions Zara might be kept in, or for how long, if they did not catch Jalal tonight.

The air was strangely damp, and the sound of the horse's hooves echoed. They were moving slightly downhill. Zara strained her ears, trying to take in every detail of what she heard, in case it might later prove useful. Was it a cave? If so, it was a very large one, and she was sure they had not been riding towards the mountains. An underground cavern? The thought that it might be her prison made her shiver. The horse seemed to pick its way in darkness.

After a long time measured only by the beating of her terror, the dampness lifted and their path went uphill again. Then the horse whickered softly, and there was a voice.

Her captor called out, and the voice answered, and now through her makeshift blindfold she saw the glow of light. The horse stopped, and her captor called soft commands, and she was lifted from the horse and carried.

She didn't scream or struggle. Better to give them no excuse, she thought. Not that they would need one.

Rafi cursed himself. He would never buy a civilian helicopter again. There was no infrared, no night search capability besides the feeble landing light. And the whole desert to search. They radioed the nearest military camp to scramble a couple of Sikorskys, but Rafi knew in his heart the task was now impossible. They had given him time to get to cover. Jalal was not such a fool as to go on riding through the desert with a captive woman all night long.

And even if he did, he was not the only rider in the desert. They might stop half a dozen riders abroad on legitimate—and illegitimate—business on a night of full moon like tonight.

But he searched, all the same. Once they reached the hard ground he saw the extent of the task, for the man might have gone anywhere from here and left no trace. There were thousands of trails across the desert.

At dawn, ordering the search to continue, he returned to the palace and went alone to his study. He sat in thought, but thinking would not change anything. Prince Jalal's ransom demand would come soon enough. Before that, if possible, his brothers must be warned.

"Ah, he chooses well, Prince Rafi!" said the bandit, his teeth very white against his dark beard.

They had set her on her feet by a roaring fire. Her heart-beat was stifling her. "He has not chosen me for anything," Zara said. "I am a member of a Canadian archaeological team and believe me, the Canadian government—"

He laughed. "We heard that Prince Rafi had followed in the steps of Khosrow and fallen in love with a woman bathing. Do not deny that it is you. I saw you with a robe of such value that only he could have given it to you. And I saw your beauty. By moonlight I thought you a Peri. By firelight also your beauty enchants."

She was in a strange compound, that seemed to be surrounded by rocks and ancient ruins. But the fire blinded her. She could not see much beyond it. There were people in the distance moving to and fro, as if going about their regular business. Where could she be?

"He gave everyone on the team a robe," she said dismissively. Zara felt sick at heart. He looked so like Prince Rafi! How could such a startling resemblance be coincidence? What did it mean? "We have found the lost city of Alexander. Prince Rafi has no personal interest in me at all."

The dark face closed. "If it is true, that is a pity for you."

Five

FROM JALAL IBN AZIZ TO HIS SERENE HIGHNESS RAFI IBN DAUD: I HAVE YOUR WOMAN. NO HARM WILL COME TO HER IF YOU AND YOUR BROTHERS OMAR AND KARIM AGREE TO MEET WITH ME AND HEAR MY DEMANDS.

"The fault is all mine!" Rafi said. Prince Karim and Prince Omar had arrived for a council of war. "In the first place, I should have had guards posted."

"True enough," said Omar dispassionately. "Why didn't you?"

"Because I was besotted by black curls, like the excellent Khosrow," Rafi said.

Karim nodded. "We heard. You came back from a ride and put the whole palace on alert for a grand feast in the desert. It was said you had seen a woman bathing in the Wadi Sahra and lost your mind. Your cooks worked flat out for three days."

"Word travels, doesn't it?" Rafi said.

"When a prince loses his marbles there's always someone with access to a phone."

"Well, I don't deny it. I've found her, and now because of me she's in danger. Worse. If I hadn't—and if we hadn't disagreed with you, Omar, about how dangerous Jalal would become, we might have dealt with him ages ago."

"We'll deal with him now," Omar said.

They had agreed that the tribes would see it as a sign of weakness if they submitted to Jalal's demands.

"I admit I was hoping to plan my wedding before undertaking a desert campaign. But Jalal comes first now," Omar added.

"Do we know where he's taken her?"

"I've got half the army out scouring the desert for any sign, but one thing is certain—he's on this side of the river. He didn't cross the Dar al Jenoub bridge—we had that closed off before he had any chance of reaching it. And now with your men monitoring the other bridges…and there have been no unscheduled aircraft flights anywhere in the area."

"So he had a place chosen in East Barakat."

"And until my men stumble on it, there's only one way to find out where that is," Rafi said.

His brothers looked at him expectantly. "Send someone to infiltrate Jalal's camp to listen for clues. Someone there knows where she's being held."

Karim and Omar nodded silently. "Yeah, sounds good," said Karim after a moment. "Who will you send?"

"Myself," said Rafi.

FROM HIS SERENE HIGHNESS SAYED HAJJI RAFI JEHANGIR IBN DAUD IBN HASSAN AL QURAISHI, PRINCE OF EAST BARAKAT, TO THE BANDIT JALAL: WE OFFER NOTHING AND ACCEDE TO NO DEMANDS. WE URGE YOU TO GIVE UP YOUR HOSTAGE INSTANTLY. REMEMBER THE SWORD OF ROSTAM. WE URGE YOU TO AVOID THE

CATASTROPHE WHICH WILL SURELY ENSUE IF YOU PER-
SIST IN YOUR PATH. WE URGE YOU TO AVOID THE FATE
OF THE SWORD OF ROSTAM. RELEASE YOUR HOSTAGE.

Zara lifted the battered tin pot for the third time in five
minutes and confirmed that there was still no water in it.

If there was one thing solitary confinement taught you,
it was how irrational the human mind really was. There
was no water in the pot, and there wouldn't be any until
the woman came and brought some, but she was thirsty and
could not control the urge to check. It did not help that by
her reckoning—which might or might not be accurate, since
she had no watch—the old woman was late. She came
every day, once during the morning and once in the late
afternoon, to bring the modicum of water and food Zara
was allowed and to empty her latrine. Other than that she
was left entirely alone.

The woman spoke no English or French, and Zara's
handful of Arabic words hadn't been designed with the
needs of a hostage in mind.

She was irritable because it was so hard to keep her mind
off her physical discomfort. She was lying in a disinte-
grating room of an ancient ruin that appeared to be the
camp of Jalal the bandit and his far from merry men. She
had been wearing the same dress for three days. The dress
had been white: there was nothing to disguise her filthy
state. That was worse than the intermittent hunger and
thirst. The dirt was a constant. Her hair was matted. The
thick walls of her prison had been designed to stay cool
during the summer heat, but still she sweated in the after-
noons. Although she mercifully could not smell herself, no
doubt she stank.

Her prison cell was doorless and empty, with collapsing
walls, and the once-beautiful tile floor was faded and broken, and gritty with desert sand that had been blowing into
the ruin for centuries. They had given her a camel blanket
to serve as both mattress and covering.

Worst of all, she was chained by the ankle to a bolt in the wall which, for all that it looked as if it had been there since Noah, was absolutely immovable. She had a range of a few feet, enough to take her from her blanket to her latrine—a tin pail mercifully covered with a thick wooden lid—in the only corner she could reach.

At least her nose and ears had not been removed, which had been standard practice for the enemies of the state under Darius, King of the Medes and Persians, in the time before Alexander came to conquer these lands. "Him I punished well," was the way Darius had recorded such events. She wondered how Jalal the bandit would record her incarceration for history, given the chance.

Two thousand five hundred years ago. She supposed she wasn't anything like as miserable as those poor rebels against the great usurper Darius had been—or even many more recent hostages—but she was uncomfortable enough.

Alexander the Great had been appalled by the Eastern treatment of prisoners. History suggested that he had been met by a group of Greek craftsmen and artisans—prisoners, who had all suffered amputations of whatever part of their anatomy was not relevant to their art, in order to prevent their escape. In those days, she supposed, potters were the lucky ones—their craft had needed both feet and hands. But painters, silversmiths, or mosaic workers would have lost their feet. Some sources said it was in revenge for these atrocities that Alexander had burned the great, magnificent palace of Persepolis, but Zara had never quite believed it....

God, if he started cutting off bits of her! It had been said that Mohammad had only countenanced such barbarity because he knew it would be useless to try to ban it completely. But fourteen hundred years later it was still the treatment of choice for some...was Jalal one of them?

Alexander. Why couldn't she entertain herself with stories of Alexander instead of frightening herself with possibilities? She moved restlessly, trying to control her thoughts, and the chain on her ankle clanked. Zara laughed, but without much real mirth. Impossible to escape from her thoughts.

She heard no warning. There was simply no one in the doorway one minute and a man standing there the next. His face was covered; he was swathed in a burnous and keffiyeh. Zara gasped in fear and struggled to her feet, her back against the broken stone wall. She cowered for a moment as the chain dragged painfully at her ankle and reminded her how helpless she was, then stiffened her courage and straightened her back.

She had tried not to imagine this moment, tried not to think that it must come. "Women will attend you," the bandit had told her grandly. "Have no fear for your virtue while you are in my protection!" She had tried not to believe that, either, knowing if she did it would only be worse if it happened. When.

"*Alhamdolillah!* Can it be you?" cried the man in a fierce whisper, and launched himself at her. He wrapped his arms around her, and she felt sickness rise in her throat, choking her. Pushing at him, she drew her head back, gasped for air to scream. But he was quick. One slim dark hand, fine and hard as steel, smothered the cry.

"Do not cry out!" he pleaded in English. "It is I!"

His other hand pulled down his scarf. Jalal the bandit himself, she thought bitterly, blinked, then stared. Smiling reassuringly, he took his hand from her mouth.

"*Prince Rafi!*" she whispered, aghast. Oh, worse, much worse than she had imagined! If she were a prisoner of the prince himself...now it all fell into place.

"I am a fool to have frightened you," he murmured. His arm still behind her back, tight across her waist, he lifted the other to stroke her hair from her face with melting tenderness. "But I was overwhelmed at seeing you. We did not think you could be here. Thank God I have found you! Are you well? How has he treated you?"

"Get away from me," Zara hissed, and fought against

his grip. "Do you think I'm a fool to be taken in by a trick like this?"

Releasing her instantly, His Serene Highness drew himself up in frowning amazement. "I am party to no trick. What is it you believe?"

"The man who kidnapped me is not Jalal the bandit," she said. "You should have chosen a conspirator who looked a little less like you, Your Highness! Who is he, really—one of your brothers? Am I supposed to faint into your arms with relief and gratitude at being rescued? Or doesn't my reaction matter too much?"

Prince Rafi eyed her with concern, then began to paw at his voluminous burnous. "I have water," he said gently, his voice still scarcely above a whisper. He pulled out a canteen. "And a little food. You are perhaps delirious with want after three days."

Furiously she knocked his hand aside. "Do you imagine I'll take anything at all from your hands? How *dare* you do this to me? Let me go!"

"Khanum?" called a voice from the passage. Prince Rafi froze.

"If they take me, we are lost," he whispered, lifting a finger to her lips, then whirled, glancing swiftly around, saw and slipped agilely through a gaping crack in the wall to the room beyond.

His reaction was so basic. Suddenly she was convinced. His life depended on her not giving away his presence here. Zara sank down onto her haunches and picked up the empty water pot. "I need water!" she cried in the same tone she had used to the prince, banging the pot on the ground for good measure. "How dare you leave me to starve?"

The frightened old woman slipped in through the doorway and murmured incomprehensible apologies. Zara gazed balefully at her. "Water!" she commanded. *"Ma'!"* She had learned the word quickly.

"Ma'," the old woman agreed, smiling and gesturing, and lifted the small earthenware jug she was carrying. Be-

tween her clothing, her sun-scored skin and the jug, she was a timeless figure. Probably she hadn't changed much since Alexander was here, Zara thought, watching the water trickle invitingly into her little pot. There was never enough water in the jug the woman brought, and she never seemed to understand Zara's attempts to convince her to carry a bigger one. Perhaps Jalal had given orders to limit what she got.

Zara snatched up the pot and drank thirstily, and the woman obligingly refilled it again with the last of what she had. That, Zara knew, had to last her the next twelve hours or so. The old woman reached into a pocket of her robe and pulled out a cake, which she placed in Zara's hungry hand with another smile and muttered word.

"*Shokran.* Thank you," Zara said, between bites, and the woman bowed, nodding, picked up the latrine bucket, and was gone.

Her chain did not allow her to reach the wall through which he had gone. "Are you still there?" Zara whispered between bites. Now she was desperate to know he had not gone and left her alone.

Prince Rafi slipped back into her cell and stood waiting in silence as she wolfed down the strange little cake. It tasted like a cross between wheat and potatoes, flavoured with unknown spices.

"It doesn't compare to a meal in your tent," she said dryly when she had finished, a little embarrassed to have shown such hunger in front of another human being. "But it's better than starving."

"Much better," he agreed gently, and suddenly she was no longer embarrassed. "I am sorry that you suffer for the troubles of my country. We should have dealt with this vandal long ago. My brother Omar said so, and we did not listen. It is my fault that you are here, and I will get you out."

He stepped to the door and looked through while Zara tried not to drink more of the water in the pot. "You are

not guarded? Jalal must be very sure of his perimeter de-
fences to mount no internal guard on this ruin.''

Zara shook her head, though he had his back to her. ''No,
only that woman comes—usually twice a day.'' She took
another tiny sip. ''Otherwise I haven't seen anyone.'' Suddenly remembering, she gasped and said, ''She'll be back
in a minute with my...with the bucket. You should hide.''

He obediently turned back and went through the wall,
and a moment later she heard the old woman's step.

He was back with her again soon after the old woman
left. He pulled out his canteen again, unscrewed the cap,
and offered it to her without a word. Taking it with a little
murmur of gratitude, Zara drank her fill for the first time
in three days, and gave a long sigh of relief. Her hand was
wet, and not to waste a drop, she wiped it across her dusty
face. It was sharply, deliciously cooling.

''Oh, that is so good!'' she said.

He was pulling something from another pocket and she
watched him like a hungry cat. ''Dried dates,'' he said.
''Desert food.''

After three days without sugar in any form, she found
them surprisingly sweet. ''Thank you!'' she said, her voice
cracking. ''Thank you so much for coming!''

Tears of gratitude, hot as acid, burned her eyes. She saw
how terrible a punishment solitary was...to be cut off from
all human interaction had shaken her to the core. She had
not understood how deeply she was affected till this moment. She hungered to touch him, to be held and comforted,
to be reassured that she was a valued member of the human
race. It was as hard to fight as the need for water.

He did not wait for her to ask. When she ate another
date and began to cry in earnest over its precious sweetness,
he cradled her in his arms, pressing her head to his shoulder. ''Cry, my dear one,'' he soothed her. ''Cry first, and
then we will discuss the future.''

She could not resist, but stood sobbing against him, while

a wave swept her—the release of pent-up fear and anguish that she had not allowed herself to feel before.

He felt the sobs tear at her, her struggles to keep them silent. He did not know what suffering her tears covered. Imprisonment, of course, that was natural enough, but…she had said no one came, no one hurt her, she had seen no one save the old woman. And yet…

"If he has hurt you, Beloved, believe that you shall be avenged ten times over," he promised, choking back sorrow and rage.

If she had been harmed, nothing would prevent Rafi from spilling the bandit's lifeblood, every ounce, into the sand of the desert he pretended to own. He would make her his wife and his queen regardless—nothing could prevent that except her own wish…but he would kill the bandit first, without mercy; he would cut his heart from his breast and hurl it to the dogs, if she had been hurt.

The rush of relief was terrible to him—as primitive as birth and death—when she shook her head resolutely against his breast. "No. He said he wouldn't, and I haven't seen a man since I got here. That was why I thought you…" she whispered through her tears, and broke off to sob again. "Please don't kill him on my behalf."

"Beloved, I cannot swear to spare this bandit's life," Rafi said. "But his death will not be laid at your door."

He stroked her hair tenderly, and murmured soothing words to her in his own tongue, the soft music of which she found comforting. Her sobs subsided quickly; she was resilient, and she drew back and smiled up at him.

"Now," he said. "We must talk. Every moment is precious. Sit, and tell me all that you know. Tell me first how you were brought here. We did not think to find you here. We thought you still on the other side of the river."

She stared at him. "What do you mean? What side of the river am I on?"

He helped her to sit, and pulled up his burnous to reveal desert boots, jeans, and a hip holster, from which he pulled a gun. Then he sat beside her, leaning against the ancient wall, and drew her against his shoulder with his left arm while he cradled the gun in his right and watched the door.

"We are in my brother Omar's territory, Central Barakat. You were not aware of being brought across the river?"

"No! Are you sure? Oh, sorry, how stupid! Of course you're sure. But I think I'd have realized."

"Were you drugged at any time?"

"Never—well, not so far as I know. Anyway, not while he had me on the horse, and he brought me straight here, we didn't make any stops. I thought it was going to kill the horse."

"How long did you ride?"

"Hours. I lost track."

He watched her. "You travelled for hours and you arrived at this place without crossing the river?"

Zara nodded. "After a long time he made me blindfold myself, and then I thought he was taking me into an underground cavern, or something. It was very damp. There was water dripping, and I could hear wind roaring at a distance. I was terrified he was going to tie me up deep underground. But then there was light, and voices, and we were here. By that time it was almost dawn, but I was put in this room before I saw much. Is this his headquarters? I thought he must have moved them."

He was frowning with thought, and nodded absently. "How can this be?" After a moment, his brow cleared. "What can you remember of where you were before you were forced to put on the blindfold?"

"I—oh! I almost forgot! I dropped...threw down that beautiful gold robe you gave me, just before we went inside, I think. I hoped it was, but maybe we were already in the cave.... I thought the helicopter searchlight might pick up the glitter. I'm sorry, was it very valuable?"

"It will never be more valuable than as a marker. We must send out parties to search for it, and solve this mystery."

"My sandals too. I did think I saw one of those big piles of rock in the distance when he blindfolded me, and I thought I heard running water," Zara contributed, as her memory came back. "But I couldn't tell whether we went towards it or not after I was blindfolded."

Still thinking, taking it in, Rafi nodded. "What else, my beloved? What other clues have you? For I must go. Time is passing."

She said doubtfully, "Do you know that you and Jalal look alike?"

"No, though you said it a moment ago. Is it a strong likeness?"

He turned and his black eyes fixed hers, reminding her, and doubt crept over her again. She had only his word for anything—only his word that she was on the Central Barakat side of the river. Didn't captors try to disorientate their captives in order to break them down mentally?

He understood directly what she was thinking, as if the thoughts were in his own head. Rafi shook his head at the great mystery. Had not his father often spoken of knowing his beloved wife's thoughts?

"Do not mistrust me," he urged her softly. "A moment of doubt at a critical moment and all may be lost. You can, and you must, trust me absolutely, now and forever. I am your husband. You are my wife. There can be no room between us for doubt."

Six

She felt the silence enter her soul. "What are you talking about?" she asked in a level voice.

Rafi drew back a little to look at her more closely, there in the circle of his arm. "You have not felt it? You do not yet know?" he asked.

She looked at him wordlessly. She was sure of nothing. She was so disorientated—could this all be part of a good-cop bad-cop routine? Was he going to try to convince her that she had amnesia or something?

He smiled into her suspicious, doubting eyes. "I knew it in the moment that I looked at you. My father also knew like this, in one blow, when he saw my stepmother for the first time. He saw his fate. It has been so for me. Of course you do not feel it now, here in a prison—your mind is too full of other things. But you almost felt it that night, as you sat beside me—I know that the knowledge was close to you then. Is it not so?"

With all her might, Zara resisted. She had to look away

from his dark, entrancing, love-certain eyes. "If it was true that you loved me, you would not take advantage of this situation."

She felt it go through him like a little shock. "You are right," he said. Gently he lifted his arm and took it away, and she felt her loss so keenly her eyes burned. She bit her lip on the retraction that almost burst from her. She was certain of nothing, and she was vulnerable. Very vulnerable.

"Now," he said, in a more businesslike tone.

"How did you get in here?" Zara pressed. "Aren't there armed guards?"

Rafi nodded. "We stopped the truck of a man from the village who brings in supplies. We thought he might know where you were being kept, but he swore he had not been asked to take his vegetables and meat anywhere save here." He shrugged. "We took his brother hostage, and I came inside in place of the brother."

"Why?"

"Why? To find news of you. I hoped to hear talk of where you were being kept. We did not dream that you were here." Rafi paused. "He is a fool to have brought you here. When I heard one of the women call to another that she would soon take the prisoner food and water, I did not dare to hope it could be you."

His voice was soothing her, making it difficult for her to concentrate. Zara shook her head, trying to clear it. It was so hard to keep her suspicions high, and yet she was sure she should. She had no idea whether it was plausible or not. At the dig they were supplied by such an arrangement as the prince described, by one of the local villagers in his battered truck...but what did that prove? Perhaps only that Prince Rafi knew his story would be convincing.

Before she could decide what to answer, he was on his feet. "My brothers are waiting for me in the desert, where they hold the villager hostage. I must leave with the truck. Do not lose hope. We will free you before long."

She struggled to her feet, and, without meaning to, wailed, "You're *leaving?*"

Of course he could not resist the tone of despair and longing. He bent and swiftly kissed her mouth. "I swear to return," he whispered.

It was their first kiss, and each felt the sudden fire of the connection. Rafi smiled, his teeth looking very white in the gloom, and restored his gun to the holster. He picked up her hand, and bent to kiss it. "I will come to you soon, my beloved."

Rafi moved quickly through the empty rooms of the fortress ravaged by time and Genghis Khan and crept through the shadows till he was close to where the now nearly empty truck stood. To his dismay, all the buying was finished. There was only one woman still standing with the driver. He strode out into the open, where he began a tuneless whistling as he slung an empty crate onto the pile of empties on the truck bed. He was surprised at the amount of food that had been offloaded. Jalal's band of rebels must be bigger than any of them had guessed.

The villager threw him a look of mingled fear and relief, set down the glass of mint tea with a word of thanks to the woman who had offered it, and signalled to him to get into the truck. Rafi wordlessly climbed into the cab.

"Is your stomach very bad?" cried the old woman to him. He had used his sick stomach as an excuse to ask for a toilet. But he had been gone a long time. Too long.

He was afraid to say too much in the desert accent. "Thank you, Mother," he said, shaking his head.

"You should have some mint tea, that will settle a sick stomach," she cried.

"Next time," he muttered, smiling.

The vegetable supplier slammed the truck noisily into gear and turned towards the gate.

"I told her my brother was sick with the same thing, that I had asked you my cousin to help but you were no better, with a stomach like a woman's. I drank four cups of tea, as a preventative. I thought you would never come back," he said, in frightened irritation.

He did not know who his passenger was, nor the partners who held his own brother hostage, but he had seen the bandit Jalal many times, and his passenger's likeness to him behind the keffiyeh was not reassuring. If he was on the wrong side of an internecine struggle, it would go badly for him and his family when whatever was coming was over—and a man who was on both sides was sure of only one thing: being on the wrong side.

Both men sighed with relief as the guard at the gate waved the truck through without incident.

"The tunnel. The tunnel of Queen Halimah," breathed Omar. "Is it possible?" They sat in silence for a moment, absorbing the thought. "It would explain why my siege of the place never had any effect. They could bring anything they wanted in through the tunnel."

"I've always thought that story was a myth," said Karim. "Every old ruin of a public works is attributed to Queen Halimah."

Rafi said, "Just because she's become a legend doesn't mean there isn't some truth to the stories. Zara wasn't taken across a bridge. She's on the other side of the river. How else did he get her there?"

Karim shrugged apologetically. "A woman who has just been taken hostage isn't necessarily in the best frame of mind for making acute observations."

"You're speaking from experience, of course," Omar returned. Karim flushed.

"There is nothing wrong with Zara's mental capacity," Rafi said quickly. "She said she wasn't taken across a bridge and I believe her. Anyway, the alternative requires not only that she was hallucinating, but that our soldiers screwed up at the bridges. The alternative is simpler. I think he's found a tunnel."

Omar said quietly, "I agree. Look at the archaeological dig. Your archaeologist is the first one to take the old stories about the change in the river's course seriously, and as a result he found the lost city of Iskandiyar." Omar lit a black cigarette and drew on it thoughtfully. "And there's a direct connection, isn't there? Because the story suggests that the course of the river was changed in order to build a tunnel under it. Queen Halimah had a tunnel built and then moved the river to flow over it, isn't that the archaeologist's idea?"

Rafi, who had heard it all at impassioned length from Gordon at the time of giving permission for the dig, nodded. "That's about it."

"We need to consult him on this. He must have done aerial photography of the whole area when he was looking for Iskandiyar," Omar continued. "Maybe they'll show something."

"We also have Zara's help," Rafi said, and told them about the golden robe. "I want to get the men to work searching for that robe."

His brothers stared at him. "It'll be covered with sand, if not blown away entirely," Karim said. "It's been four days."

"They'll find it somewhere," Rafi insisted quietly. "Don't give up till they have."

Omar frowned. "What are you going to be doing meanwhile?"

"I'm going back into Jalal's camp."

There was a startled silence. Omar squinted at him through the smoke. "You can't do it," he began.

Karim jumped in. "You're crazy, Rafi! What good will it do if you're taken prisoner, too?"

"I don't intend to be taken prisoner. She's being kept in an isolated part of the ruined fortress and there are plenty of places to hide."

"I still think we should just roll up with tanks and smash through the main gate," Karim said.

"She is chained to a wall in a ruin. Even artillery fire could bring the place down on her head. Mortar certainly would," Rafi told him. "I am going to get her free before we make any attempt to storm the place, and that is not open to discussion."

Karim turned to Omar. "He's crazy. Don't you think he's crazy? We can't let him do it."

The cigarette dropped to the sand, and Omar's boot absently crushed it in. He looked at Karim and shrugged. "It's his woman, Karim. What would you be saying right now if it were Caroline?"

Karim started to say something, stopped, thought for a moment, and shook his head in resignation.

"There's no time to argue. We've got to get organized. I want to go back in with some equipment and supplies. We have to work out how to get me in there. And we have to make contingency plans, and work out a signalling system, because once in I may not get out again," said Rafi.

She lived in perpetual shadow. The light in her prison was diffused, creeping in through the cracks between the stones, spilling in from the passage outside, with more or less intensity, depending on the time of day. Zara lay and watched the sunlight retreat through the door and down the passage, until she was in the near darkness that she knew would last till morning. Sometimes the firelight reached her, but more usually it appeared only as flickering shadows.

She was being swept by feelings over which she seemed to have no control. Sometimes she loved Rafi so fiercely it hurt. From these deep feelings of trust and longing she would be swept to feelings of terrible doubt. Everything he had said and done came under the review of a hard, frightened little voice in her: how was it Jalal and he looked so much alike? And why was he ignorant of that fact....? And how had he found her cell? He had said he heard two women talking about taking her water, but Rafi had arrived *before* the old woman with the water.

Those and a thousand other doubts tormented her, like flies buzzing around her head. And there was no reality check in a place like this. She had nothing but her own mind, and her mind at the moment was a sea of chaos with hardly a spar in sight.

Would he come back, or was it a trick?

If he did come back, should she trust him?

At last she wrapped herself in the dirty blanket and fell asleep on her hard bed to dream confused dreams. She awoke, as usual, in the night. Hunger and thirst and discomfort disturbed her sleep, but now she felt that something had awakened her. She sat up, leaning against the wall, and listened for a moment, but there was only silence.

"Rafi?" she whispered.

Suddenly there was the sound of an explosion, and the passage wall outside her cell glowed a faint red for a moment. Then there was the crackle of gunfire, and she heard shouts and calls, and more gunfire. Explosions, and the sounds of galloping horses, the high ululating cry of raiders.

For several minutes, her heart beating crazily with fear and uncertainty, Zara sat listening to the sounds of attack. Nameless terrors rushed through her head: if everyone who knew she was here was killed, would she be left to starve and die? Who were the attackers? What if they found her? How would she be treated? As a freed hostage, or as a spoil of war?

It was over quickly. The horse hooves faded into the distance, the last shots were fired, the uncomprehending screams of women were silenced, the random flickering light changed to utter darkness. A man shouted incomprehensibly for a few minutes and then all was silent.

Zara stood waiting. All she could hear now was her own anguished heartbeat. Wild thoughts occurred to her like cuts from an invisible whip. What had happened? Were they alive or dead out there? Suppose it had been a chemical attack? She was so powerless here, chained to the wall like a dog, to be forgotten or remembered at someone's whim…should she call out or remain silent? What was safer?

She saw the glimmer of a distant light reflected on the wall of the passage outside the door. She watched it without breathing. She had never seen a light there at night before; no one ever came to her cell during the hours of darkness, but somehow she knew that this was the light of a lantern approaching her.

Footsteps, and then the lantern was in the doorway, held high. She saw the dark eyes, and almost cried his name aloud. She bit it back for a split second, and then noticed the beard.

"You are well?" said Jalal the bandit.

Her breath hissed between her teeth. Thank God she had not called Rafi's name! Her heart had never beat so wildly in her life. Sick fear invaded her. What was he going to do? She needed a delaying tactic, needed to get him talking…

"What happened?" she asked.

His eyes glittered as they raked her, seeking the answer to some question. "A small harassing campaign—it is nothing. A few men from one of the desert tribes, perhaps, looking for easy pickings, hoping to find our guards asleep. Or perhaps not."

She stared at him.

"Perhaps it was your lover, the prince. He may have hoped to judge our strength and readiness from our response to such a raid. What do you think?"

"Or maybe he planted a bomb inside the camp. Maybe it will go off when you least expect it." She stood wrapped in her blanket, her eyes wide in the lantern light. He was reminded suddenly of a small, trapped animal, delicate, beautiful, but capable of very fierce resistance if attacked.

"Do not be afraid of me," he said suddenly. "You are in no danger here. My men obey me."

"Then why are you keeping me?" she managed to ask over the lump of terror in her throat.

Jalal grinned, showing his teeth like a fierce wild animal that smiles as a warning. "You are the bait in my trap to draw the princes of Barakat. They will come to me—of this you may be sure."

"They'll come and kill you, I'm sure of that."

He smiled and shook his head. "They cannot kill me. They know it."

His confidence could only be braggadocio. If she could keep him talking about the magic that made him invincible.... "Really?" she asked in bright curiosity, as if they were at a cocktail party. "Why not? What makes you invincible?"

He grinned again. "Ask your lover, Prince Rafi, the next time you see him! He will tell you! You have food, water?"

Taken aback by the sudden question, Zara nodded dumbly.

"It is good." To her amazement he bowed and swept out.

It was useless to lie down. She was wide awake with nerves. She sat waiting for her eyes to grow accustomed to the darkness again, thinking. She wished he had left her the lantern. The night was friendlier when you had light.

As if the thought gave rise to a hallucination, she saw the flickering glow of a light, not from the passage, but from that gap in the wall opposite that led to a room beyond.

"He never thought you would be able to respond to his parting advice so quickly as this," Prince Rafi murmured, sticking his head and the candle through the wall and smiling at her, "but since I'm here, you may as well take advantage of my presence, don't you think?"

Seven

"**P**rince Rafi!" she whispered, and threw herself towards him. The chain around her ankle pulled her up short so that she fell forward, but he dropped the candle and swooped to catch her in his arms. Relief overwhelmed her.

The candle lay burning in the dust as his mouth found hers. Zara trembled as his passion enclosed her. Her heart yearned towards him, she felt both tears and laughter in her blood, and the complete conviction that she had come home at last.

His mouth was cool and warm at the same time, his tongue delicious, his hold both tender and ruthless, his body accommodating hers like the softest bed, and yet so strongly muscled. When their mouths parted she lay in his arms, and felt his lips tremble along her throat, her cheek, her forehead, her hair, felt her own response to the loving touch swamp her, drown her, move her almost unbearably to tears and joy.

"Beloved," he was murmuring. "My beloved."

The candle flame gave a last flicker in the dust and went out. This broke through the spell, and she reluctantly drew away. She was so vulnerable here, both mentally and physically. Between one moment and the next, she had become desperate for his company, his touch, considered him her saviour.… She knew such things happened in situations like this. Hostages fell in love with their captors. Judgement got lost.

Her emotions were so near the surface—she had never before experienced anything like what she felt now around Prince Rafi. It frightened her, because what else could it be but the peculiar madness of being held hostage?

He didn't attempt to keep his hold on her, but bent and snatched up the candle while the glow of the wick still announced its whereabouts. Zara heard the click of a lighter, and then the candle flame flared up again.

"Oh, how lovely to have light!" she exclaimed involuntarily. "It's so beautiful, candlelight!" And again, the softness of it, the tenderness of that fragile flame in a dark world brought her close to tears.

He stood before her, holding the candle up and looking at her by its light, much as the bandit had done, and with the same dark, flashing eyes. But for all that, there was a world of difference in his gaze. She would never mistake them for more than a fleeting moment. "Come," he murmured. "Let us sit."

She allowed him to guide her to where her blanket lay crumpled, and stood passively holding the candle while he folded it and placed it neatly on the ground. They sat and Rafi carefully spilled a little wax and fixed the candle on the ground between them.

"Now," he said.

Questions tumbled over themselves in her mind. "You came back," she said wonderingly. "How did you do it? Was that your men who made the attack tonight?"

"Not my men, but my brothers, and my Cup Companions, and theirs."

"Your brothers? All three of you?" she repeated. "But what if you'd all been killed?"

He shook his head. "We did not think it likely. In any case, most of the noise and light was caused by fireworks." He tapped the stone wall they were leaning against with one knuckle. "This structure is not so sturdy that we could risk real mortar. We fired some mortar out into the desert as if we had bad aim, then my brothers rode up with the Companions firing and making as much noise as possible, and I slipped in as the guards all moved to counter the assault they expected. Instead of attacking, they rode past."

He was so clean. He smelled of soap and aftershave. Zara inhaled the delightful odour of him, and was abruptly aware of her own condition.

"I'm very dirty," she said. "I know I smell horrible, and my hair is so matted—I wish I had a comb, even!"

Rafi looked into her eyes and said, "Your smell is intoxication to me, and your hair a bed of delight." She shivered with longing.

"But since you are unhappy…" Rafi leaned a little to one side and slipped his hand into the pocket of his black jeans, which he wore with a loose white shirt and the same enveloping white keffiyeh around his head that Jalal and his men wore. He was dressed like one of them.

What he pulled out was a small velvet box. He offered it to her on his palm.

Zara frowned wonderingly. "But what is it?"

"It is for you," he only said. "Take it."

She took the box, marvelling at the velvet's smoothness to the touch after days of feeling the rough blanket, and grit and hard stone.

It was a ring. A ring to dream of, a ring to die for. A huge deep green cabochon-cut emerald encircled by gleaming, glittering diamonds, rubies, sapphires. It caught the candle's glow, magnifying and intensifying it, so that she seemed to look through the ring into a starry sky.

"Ohhhh," breathed Zara. She could find no words. "How beautiful." She raised her eyes to his. "But—"

Rafi lifted his hand to stop the words on her lips. "This is a wishing ring," he said. "No more, no less. Rub the ring, and make a wish, and it will give you your desire."

She smiled, caught like a child by the promise of magic. "Really? Whatever I ask for? Suppose I ask to be free?"

"Some wishes take longer than others, but all are granted," Rafi assured her. "Put it on, and make a wish."

It was large, fitting her middle finger, where it made her hand look as if it belonged to some Eastern potentate's favourite. "What will happen when I rub it? Will a genie appear?"

"The genie is already here." He bowed. "Rub the ring, my lady, close your eyes tight, and name your wish."

She laughed aloud, for the first time in days, and instantly choked it back, reminded of her surroundings. Laughter carried like no other sound. Her heart soared. "All right!" she said, closing her eyes to concentrate and carefully rubbing the ring. "I wish I had a comb!"

Rafi raised his arms in the air, waving his hands, and said, "Abracadabra! You may open your eyes, my lady!"

On his palm lay a neat, wide-toothed comb. Zara gasped with delight and reached for it. "You have one! How did you know?"

"But the ring is magic, lady," he said, his eyes flashing with love and humour. "I of myself know nothing. Shall I comb your hair for you?"

Entranced by the look in his eyes, she passed the comb back to him. Rafi took it, picked up a lock of her matted hair, and began tenderly working the comb through it.

"Madam, shall the genie tell you a story while he combs your hair?"

Zara sighed, feeling his hands in her hair, feeling how the shock of his touch travelled to her scalp and her skin. How her prison had been transformed! Just in this moment, she thought, if freedom meant she would not see him again, she would not change places with anyone.

"Oh, yes, tell me a story!"

"Turn your back, so that I can reach, please," he said. She turned, and crossed her legs under her, pulling the slit skirt of the once-white dress up around her hips and knees.

Behind her, his voice began, "Once upon a time, long ago, there lived a great king. Mahmoud of Ghazna was his name. This king had a beautiful Turkish slave, Ayaz. Ayaz was a faithful and very beloved slave, whose hair was a special glory. It was long, and curling, and tumbled down the slave's back like a thousand black narcissus blooms, and it seemed that even the candlelight was ensnared in the fragrant net of curls."

His voice was hypnotic, and his hands worked through her curls as he spoke, so that Zara was uncertain whether it was present or past that he spoke of. His touch caused tremors to ripple over her body—shivery, delicious little tremors that put her in a kind of trance.

"The slave was forbidden to the king, and the king knew it and strove to live by the law. But one night, the king drank more than usual, and in the gentle haze he looked and saw the black hair, ringlet upon ringlet, 'in every ringlet a thousand hearts and under every lock a hundred thousand souls,' and desire filled him. He felt his approach to danger, and cried out to the slave, 'Your hair leads me astray from the path of virtue! Cut it off so that it will cease to tempt me!' and he handed Ayaz a knife.

"Ayaz, as perfect in obedience as in beauty, picked up the knife and merely asked, 'How short shall I cut it, Lord?'

"'Cut off half of it,' said the poor king.

"And instantly the slave lifted the ends of those magnificent curls onto the roots, put the knife into the fold, and cut. The king praised such devotion, drank more wine, and fell asleep.

"But in the morning!" Rafi went on, still working his deft way through the tangles of her hair. "When the slave appeared to the king for the first time, shorn of those beautiful locks, how the king was miserable, and angry with himself and all the world for what he had commanded to be done. He sank into a gloom, getting up and sitting down again and approachable by no one.

"Then his Cup Companions and his courtiers began to worry, for a king who is unhappy with himself may be a risk to others. So they wondered among themselves what could be done to bring the king back into his own good graces. At last, they went to the great poet Unsuri. 'Compose a poem that will pacify the king, and recite it to him,' they begged.

"And so Unsuri went in to the king, who said to him, 'Well, say something about this.' And being a great poet, Unsuri immediately composed a poem."

"What was the poem?"

He recited it to her in a haunting, rhythmic voice not unlike the sounds made by Motreb on the night of the feast.

"That sounds magical," she said with a smile. "I feel better, and I don't even know what it means!"

"It has been attempted by several translators over the past nine hundred years. Literally, it means, 'It may be a crime to have cut a few of the curls of such an idol of beauty, but what's the point of this restless gloom? Instead you should call for wine and wassail, and be of good cheer. A cypress is most decorative when it has been trimmed!'"

Zara wrinkled her nose a little in disappointment. He was quick to catch it. "Yes, the poem in the original is more than its meaning. A modern poet has done it better justice. Shall I recite that?"

She nodded.

He began to recite with a more pronounced rhythm than she was used to hearing in English. It was seductive.

> "whisper of ambergris through the cut of beauty
> against the curve of spine, deep swathe and coal
> his eyes in faint of length and glow

on a nape of hyacinth and honey
unravelling knots swallowed sweet and long
holding too much in the billow

although scissor slips of shame find an unsettled dawn,
watch, and call for wine,
as the strong green cypress winds radiant

clipped only this morning.''

His voice was rich, deep, taking the poem personally. She felt his eyes on her own neck, on the billow of her hair, and every word was charged.

When he finished they sat in silence, while Rafi drew the comb long and straight through her untangled hair.

''That's…lovely,'' she breathed at last. She liked poetry, but she'd never once met a man who would so unselfconsciously recite it. Or admit to sharing a poet's feeling.

''Yes,'' he said, and he meant more than the poem.

''So, do you want me to cut my hair off?'' she said with a smile, fighting to loosen the grip of the dangerous mood.

Rafi dropped the comb and laughed. ''Never!'' He drew his hands down through the full length of her hair from crown to below her waist, and lifted it to fall in a glittering wave in the candlelight.

Zara swung around to face him, and took the comb as he offered it to her. She drew it through her hair for the pleasure of feeling how neat it was again, her head tilting so that her face was half hidden from him. ''Doesn't it tempt you from the path of virtue?''

He sat up and took her wrist, stopping the hypnotic, rhythmic motion. ''Your hair tempts me, yes. It incites me to desire, with many other things about you. But you are not a slave, and you are not forbidden to me. It is marriage that I think of. You know this. I have said it.''

She dropped her head further, veiling her face completely, and made no answer. There was a moment's silence. Against his hand she felt his heartbeat and her own, two separate strands, and listened while they merged for a few powerful synchronous beats, then parted again, like the different threads of a melody.

They sat for a long, silent moment, both of them listening to the music of their hearts. Then Zara yawned, but whether from nerves or fatigue she didn't know. One of the worst torments of her imprisonment was not being able to sleep soundly, but in Rafi's presence she was miles from feeling sleepy.

"It is time you slept," he said.

"Is it very late?" she asked.

"Very," he agreed. "Nearly three."

She was surprised. She had thought it around midnight. She felt that she could have sat talking to him for hours yet. But she knew he would have to leave the camp again before dawn.

"How are you going to get out again?"

Rafi smiled. "I will get out again when I take you with me. This requires a plan, which it has not been possible to make without knowing more about the setup here. First I must locate the tunnel that connects this camp to the other side of the river. Then when we have worked out a plan, I will communicate it to my brothers."

She stared. "You—what are you saying? You can't *stay* here!"

"Why not?"

"Because…well, it's obvious! They'll catch you!"

He smiled. "You will learn to have more faith in your husband than this."

Zara fell silent. There were a million responses to this, but she could not find the one that fit.

"But we will not plan yet. Make another wish on your wishing ring," Rafi commanded, "and then we shall sleep."

"Really?"

"What do you most wish for?"

"A toothbrush!" she said.

Rafi inclined his head. "It shall be done, lady. And what else?"

She blinked and smiled her perplexity at him.

"Do not you wish for a softer bed?" he asked.

Zara's face abruptly lost its smile. "What? How can you possibly—"

"But have you not understood that I am your genie? Do you wish for a softer bed?"

She looked at him out of the corner of her eyes. "Ye-es," she said slowly.

"Then close your eyes, rub the magic ring and make a wish. Do not open them again until I tell you to do so."

A bubble of laughter escaped her. How astonishing to think that she should laugh in such a place! Oh, he changed everything! And if he really meant to stay...

Zara closed her eyes, lifted her hand, and ritually rubbed her ring. "I wish I had a softer bed," she chanted. She heard Rafi get up from her side and step across the room. When she peeked he had disappeared, she thought through the hole in the wall. She closed her eyes again.

"You may open your eyes now."

He was standing there with a roll of something. Zara gaped at him. First holding out to her a small package, he proceeded to spread the roll out on the floor against the wall. It was a sheet of foam rubber, two inches deep, about two feet by six, grey like the stones behind the decorative tiles that had once covered the floor completely.

"I don't believe it!" she breathed. "And this—!" In her hand was a little plastic package containing a tiny toothbrush and tube of toothpaste, of the kind you found in hotels. "You really are a genie! How did—where..." The words died on her lips.

"But it is magic, my lady. You must not question the workings of magic."

He folded the blanket in two and spread it on the little

mattress. Obediently, at his command, Zara slipped between the two folds and lay down.

"Oh, what luxury! Oh, how wonderful not to feel every bone in my body!" She propped herself up on one elbow. "But where are you going to sleep?"

"Next door. It is risking too much to stay with you—we have seen tonight that someone may come at any time."

"What if someone goes into that room?"

"The doorway is a pile of rubble. Tomorrow I will build it higher. Tonight I will watch. I am well armed and there are men waiting for my signal in the desert. Sleep in the knowledge that you are safe, my beloved."

He crouched by her as she lay down again, picked up the candle and stood looking down, the tenderest of smiles in his eyes.

She was a hostage in the heart of a rebel's fortress, but she had never felt so safe, so cherished, so protected, in her life. Zara smiled up at the prince, and suddenly sleepiness crept over her. She breathed deeply, her eyes closing.

"Goodnight, sweet prince," she whispered.

She watched under drowsy, contented eyelids as the light moved away through the crack in the wall and into the next room. She watched a few minutes until it was extinguished.

She drew her hand up superstitiously and rubbed the ring. "Please keep him safe," she whispered. A moment later, still holding the ring, she was asleep.

Eight

There was a hole high up in the wall, a hole that let in one fat ray of sunlight for a few minutes every morning. Although the walls were porous, it was the only direct sunlight Zara saw, and after the first day she had moved her bed so that the beam would play on her face in the morning and wake her. Even this brief dose of sunlight was better than nothing.

Last night, Rafi had placed her new mattress in a slightly different position, and when she awoke the sunbeam was playing with the dust a few inches from her eyes. She smiled in lazy pleasure, for the moment not remembering anything, only watching the dance of the dust motes in the warm sunlight.

She had slept well. She remembered Prince Rafi first, and then where she was. With a sudden motion, she lifted her hand and saw that the ring was really there, on her middle finger. Zara smiled, stretching out her hand in the sunlight, turning the ring so that the stones caught the light and sparkled. It was exotically beautiful, and a stone that size must be worth a king's ransom.

Zara stretched and sat up, calling Prince Rafi's name in a whisper, and then a low murmur, but he did not answer. Her heart kicked nervously. Where was he? Where could he be?

But she was quick to take advantage of his absence to use the toilet. Afterwards she reached for the little dipper that held her drinking water. She always tried to save one mouthful for the mornings, to allow her to rinse her dust-dry mouth when she woke. This morning she used it to brush her teeth, and sighed for the wonder of such a simple pleasure as cleanliness.

Then she sat down on her blessedly soft bed in her ray of sunlight again and played with it until the sun climbed higher and it disappeared. That was her entertainment for the day. Usually nothing now would happen until the old woman came with her water and food.

The old woman! Zara looked down at the foam mattress. It was grey, practically invisible in the poor light, but she had no idea how sharp the old woman's eyes were. Quickly she got up and spread the blanket so that it covered the mattress as far as possible. The blanket wasn't as long as the foam, but spread on the bias, corner to corner, it covered much of it. When the woman came Zara would sit on the end that was visible.

She took off her ring, hiding it under the blanket, and settled to wait. It had been the same every day. She sat and tried to entertain herself with anything she could remember—the plot of old films, fairy tales, history, Iskandiyar, her own memories. Tried to keep the knowledge of her plight and her fears out of her mind.

Today, she found, she had an additional worry. It was not her usual nature to be nervous, it was part of the torment of imprisonment—but she was growing more and more afraid. Where was Prince Rafi? What if he had gone out for a reconnoitre or something and been caught? What would they do to him? Would Jalal recognize him? Suppose they killed him before they realized?

The old woman came at last with water and another bit of food, and Zara watched her carefully for any signs that might tell her something had occurred. But she seemed exactly like her usual self. When the woman returned for the second time with the empty pail, Zara got her attention, then put two hands up under her tilted head and mimed sleeping.

"Boom! Boom!" she said, waving her hands to indicate an explosion, opening wide eyes to indicate the sleeper's surprise.

The old woman nodded her head vigorously. "Boom!" she agreed, showing how she herself had come bolt upright in her bed. She waved her hands and made rushing noises to indicate how people had run hither and yon, and made a comment that Zara of course could not understand.

Encouraged by this willingness to communicate, Zara shot herself in the chest with her fingers and died, then lifted her hands and eyebrows to indicate a question.

The old woman shook her head. No deaths. Some hurt in the arm, or the leg, but not seriously, she indicated. Zara held up her hands in surrender, and the woman shook her head. No prisoners either.

None at all?

None.

Then the woman did a remarkable thing. She stretched out her hands to Zara, and shook her head in sad resignation, then clapped her palms together, muttering something that even across the language barrier Zara knew could be nothing other than "Poor child!"

So the woman did not approve. Zara shrugged, as if to say, What can we poor women do? The woman mirrored her shrug, and then they smiled at each other.

"Why do we do it?" Zara asked in English. "Why do we let them run the world in this ridiculous, violent way?

Bang! Bang!'' She pointed her hands like six-guns, shooting wildly at anything.

The old woman shook her head in resigned agreement, speaking in her own language. "War, always war! Never peace!" she cried, and Zara, recognizing the word *Salaamat,* understood.

So two women stood in a dusty prison and discovered understanding and agreement across the barrier of language and the arbitrary divisions of race, nationhood, creed, and politics, and knew in their hearts that, whatever surrounded them, they were not enemies.

And then one, the warder, picked up her water jug and went out, unwillingly leaving the other, her prisoner, chained like an animal to the wall.

Rafi returned soon after, whistling softly to announce his presence, and then climbing through the wall from the next room.

Zara heaved a sigh of relief. "Oh, thank God! I was getting so worried! Where have you been?"

He smiled at her in a way that turned her bones to water. "Have you been worried for me, Beloved?"

She could not imagine the term on the lips of any other man. Her eyes fell and she nodded, half-smiling.

"Do not worry. I will be safe because I must. Nothing will happen to prevent me taking you from this place."

The sweet silence of lovers fell between them. "Have you made a wish while I was away?"

She had wished for his safety, in the foolish weakness of human superstition. She did not say so, but he shook his head patiently, as if he guessed. "Wish only for yourself while you are here. What do you wish for?"

She was almost beginning to believe he could do anything, even here in the enemy camp. "A bar of soap and a cool bath," she challenged him, half believing that two Companions would march through the door with a marble tub filled with bubbles.

"Your wish is my command," intoned the genie, and slipped back through the wall. A second later he reappeared with a large pail of water. He set it down, disappeared again, and when he returned he held a facecloth and a bar of—

"Soap!" she cried, in a hoarse, happy whisper. He passed it to her and she put it to her nose, sniffing luxuriously. It was delicately, deliciously scented with almonds and patchouli. "Oh, where on earth did you find *this?*"

"It is the magic of the ring," said the genie. "There is no towel to dry you, but the air will serve as your towel. Shall the genie bathe you, Madame?"

She glinted a smile at him. "I suppose that means there's no point wishing for something to scrub my back with?"

He lifted his hands. "But no. It means that I am the back scrubber."

She didn't know why she let him do it. Prince Rafi approached her, turned her so that her back was to him, gently and deliberately lifted her hair aside and began to pull down the zipper of her dress.

It was a long zipper, extending from her neck all the way to below her waist. She heard the little cry of its passage and her skin shivered with expectation. She should stop him, should push him away, should order him out while she bathed…but she did not.

When the once-white fabric fell down around her hips, Rafi caught it and lifted it up over her head. He tossed it on her mattress without turning his eyes from her.

She was small, and perfectly formed for him, but he knew that already. She stood in the briefest of briefs, her only garment save for the black hair that fell down her back and over one shoulder like a veil.

She saw his breath catch in his chest, but he said nothing.

His eyes fell to the chain that encircled her ankle, and her own gaze followed. She could not take off her briefs over that. Yet she felt his hands in the elastic of the waist, and held her breath.

The high whisper of the tearing fabric was echoed by Zara's own indrawn breath as Rafi held the two ends of the torn silk and his muscles contracted with the effort not to touch her skin. After a moment, impersonal as a servant, he pulled the briefs down her free leg, inviting her to step out of them.

He straightened and stood looking at her again, her high beautiful breasts, sloping hips, graceful limbs, with eyes so dark with passion and control she had to part her lips to breathe.

He said in an ordinary voice, "When I take you to my palace, as I shall do as soon as I have you free, then you will have a real bath," and she was grateful for his restraint. He bent to the pail of water, dropped in the facecloth, and began to rub it with soap.

"Do you have all the modern conveniences in the palace?"

He laughed, throwing his head back, very masculine and hearty for a second until he remembered and choked it off. "In the West, of course, baths are a modern innovation. In my palace, the *hamam* has been an essential for many centuries, my beloved."

Zara blushed with embarrassment. "Pardon my cultural arrogance," she said. "I do know better."

He started with her face. Carefully, meticulously, he washed her forehead, ears, eyes, cheeks, chin, lips, neck, throat; gently rinsed and wiped them.

"Shall I describe the bath that you shall enjoy as my queen?" Rafi asked in the middle of this.

How could she protest that she would not be his queen?

He took her assent for granted. "The queen's bath chamber is quite new, only about a hundred and twenty years old. My ancestor added a large wing to the summer palace when he took a new young wife who pleased him so much that the other wives became jealous. Her name was Hala, and this part of the palace is still called Hala's wing. By tradition it belongs to the chief wife. My stepmother used it all her life, whenever we went there.''

Her shoulders, her arms, underarms, breasts and back…his touch was thrilling and hypnotic at the same time. She went into a trance of shivery yet sleepy pleasure.

"The queen's bath is a suite of rooms about ten times the size of your present chamber, my lady, and built all of the rarest marble. In some parts it is inlaid with designs in many colours. It was the work of a very fine mosaic artist, the greatest of his day. There you will see Shirin depicted bathing in a stream, and Khosrow watching her. In a long line around the walls are all his horses and men and elephants caparisoned in the most beautiful of colours, for he was on the hunt when he saw her.''

He scrubbed her hands, each finger separately, then drew her down to rinse them in the blessedly cool water. She wondered how he had gotten it, but she didn't want to speak for fear of breaking the spell. Her skin seemed to be breathing again for the first time in days, and between the luxury of that and the sensation of his electric touch, she was in heaven.

"There are other scenes, too, from tales that pleased my ancestor's young wife. Some are on the ceiling, to beguile the queen's eye while she is being massaged by the attendant, some on the walls, some on the floor of the bathing pools. History suggests that my ancestor and his young wife enjoyed bathing together. Perhaps you and I, too, will bathe there. Then I will tell you the stories that the pictures illustrate.''

He washed her stomach, abdomen, buttocks. "Your attendants will wash your body and hair, and massage you and rub rich emollient oils into your skin. Your genie has not brought any of these oils with him, my lady, because if you had all you wished here, what would tempt you to visit the palace? So some pleasures must be delayed for the sake of your lover.''

"Just the smell of this soap is heaven, at the moment," she said.

With careful deliberation, he was washing her sex. He was gentler than she could have dreamed, his touch human and personal but not sexual—and yet not denying her sexuality, either, or his own.

"When you have been massaged with the sweet-smelling oils of the *hamam,* my love, and I am beside you, your body lazy with luxury, how will you be able to resist me? If I take you then and kiss you, how will you say no to me? It would not be possible."

His voice was as sensuous as his touch. Zara's eyes were half closing where she stood, her skin rippled by wave after wave of shivery anticipation.

She thought he was waiting for something from her, but her brain was too slow now.

"No?" she asked weakly.

He smiled, as if he had had all the answer he wanted. If his touch had such power as this over her, she would be his in the end. She must be his.

"Put your foot in the pail," he commanded, and crouched down to draw the water up to her thigh with the cloth as he rubbed her, with long hypnotic strokes from thigh to shin. She rested her hand on his shoulder and lifted her foot while he scrubbed the accumulated dirt and dust from it, then she shook it dry, put it gingerly down onto the gritty floor again, and put the other foot into the water. This time she was immune to the clank of her chain.

It was blissful to immerse even just her foot in the cooling water, magic to feel so clean. But it was Rafi's touch that made her heart beat hard, his caring expertise that pulled her lips into a soft smile.

"I never expected to have my feet washed by a king," she said. "Isn't this a little out of character for you?"

He glanced up at her. "But a king is born to service."

"He is?"

"He serves his people. That is his duty. If—when you

marry me, you too will face this duty. My stepmother was a great queen. She did many things to improve the lot of the people. You will be like her. You *are* like her.''

''But I'm an archaeologist!''

''And may an archaeologist not serve the people? Perhaps we will build an important museum. Or turn the site of Iskandiyar, when you are finished there, into a tourist attraction, which will bring work to the people of the desert.''

Zara was silent with surprise. ''You've been thinking about it a lot,'' she said weakly.

''How can a man think of marrying a woman without thinking how their future will be? And how can a king give his people a queen without thinking of their welfare in his choice?''

''You have a lot of duties,'' she observed. ''Any others I should know about?''

He smiled up at her from his position at her feet. ''Every man serves his wife in the matter of physical pleasures. That also is a duty.''

''Is your life all duty, then?''

He kissed her on the side of the knee. ''God is merciful to us. Some pleasures it pleases Him to call duty.''

She had never felt the side of the knee as an erogenous zone before. That and the promise in his voice made her nerves sing. She laughed softly. ''Are you seriously telling me God calls sexual pleasure a duty?''

Rafi looked up at her in surprise. ''But of course! Do you doubt it? Are Western men such fools? The Prophet—may his name be praised!—instructed his followers not to climb on their wives like a mule, and get off again leaving her unfulfilled. 'Send a messenger first,' he said, and when they asked him what messenger, he told them, 'A kiss, a caress.' What is it you say in English?—'A word to the wise is sufficient.'''

He was finished now, and sat there on his heels, smiling up at her. ''How do you feel, my lady?''

"Very, very clean. And pampered. Thank you."

As he had said, the air had already dried her skin. "I suppose I have to get dressed again," she said ruefully, glancing down at the filthy dress with reluctance.

He shook his head in bewilderment. "But mistress," the genie protested, "have you not learned yet to use your ring?"

Zara's eyes widened with astonishment. "You—do you mean it? Really? Clean clothes?"

He shrugged. "Wish and see."

"All right." She lifted her hand and rubbed the ring, closing her eyes. She felt him silently leave her side as she did so. "I wish for clean clothes," she murmured.

She opened her eyes. The bucket, soap and cloth and her clothes were gone, and she was alone in the room. For a moment of shocking vulnerability, she thought, panicked, *What if Jalal came to see me now?* And she realized how protected Rafi's presence made her feel.

But she had no more than time to think it before Rafi was slipping back through the wall. In his hand he carried a little pile of folded white fabric. He offered it to her. On top was a neat little pair of cotton briefs, and she heaved a sigh of delight. The little puzzle of how to get them past her shackle was quickly solved—she sat and put the shackled foot through one leg, then forced the fabric up her ankle inside and past the iron. Then she could slip the other foot through and draw them up around her hips. There was nothing sexy or lacy about them, they were comfortable, well-fitting. Just what she needed.

"Oh, that feels so much better!" she exclaimed. "What else?"

She lifted up next a pair of loose white cotton pants of ingenious wrap-around design that allowed her to fold them up around her legs and tie them at the waist. Last of all came a tunic. Only when she had put it all on did she truly appreciate what he had done—the tunic reproduced the high neck and long sleeves of her dress in cool airy cotton, and the pant legs were so loose and floppy that they looked like a skirt with slits up the sides.

"But—it's almost the exact pattern of my dress!" she exclaimed. "The old woman will never see the difference in this light!" Even Jalal would probably not notice. He had seen her only in darkness, by moonlight, lamplight, firelight. "How—where did you find such a thing?"

Prince Rafi looked at her.

"Zara, I am king." He spoke gently, but she suddenly felt his power like an aura emanating from him.

Nervously, she grinned. "So you wave your hand and some minion does your bidding?"

His eyes were black suddenly. "If *you* will do my bidding when the time comes, that will be enough for me."

Nine

That night he lay with her on the narrow bed, wrapping her in his arms as they talked. She thought how strange it was that she should feel so safe in such surroundings. Not since her toddler days, when being carried on her father's shoulders, had she felt such a sense of perfect protection in the teeth of danger.

"I would like to hear you tell a story now," Rafi said.

"You're big on the idea of storytelling."

"It is an ancient and honoured tradition with my people."

Zara certainly felt she preferred this personal storytelling to television herself. "All right. What shall I tell you?" she mused.

She had not meant it as a real question, she was running over the ancient Greek tales in her head, but he took her at her word.

"Tell me about your life," he begged gently. "Let us

learn to know each other, and make up for all the time we have not spent together.''

"Oh! Where shall I start?''

"Start with the night that your father made love to your mother,'' he said, with a warm voice that traced like silk velvet on her being. "And take me from there through everything that led to your being here in my arms tonight. I want to know every detail.''

She laughed a little. No man before had ever shown such a deep interest in her. Men usually asked her about herself only as a nod to duty in between talking about themselves. "That would take a lifetime!''

"A lifetime is exactly the time we will have,'' Rafi pointed out reasonably.

She found there was no answer she could make to that. "What do you really want to know?''

"Everything. I have said.''

She wondered how long it would be before he started snoring. "Well, the way I heard it, my parents had been living together for a few years when they started to think about children.''

"What are your parents' names?'' he asked.

So he really did want full detail. "My mother's name is Maddy and my father's Brandon. So Maddy and Brandon talked it over and decided they were ready for the next step. My mother was on the pill, so she stopped taking it, and then they waited for six months for her system to normalize, and they counted dates and charted her fertility. And it wasn't exact, there was a five-day period when they should make love every day.''

"But of course,'' Rafi interjected, as if everyone in the world made love every day.

"So…the first big day—night, I guess—came, and they had champagne—please don't ask me what brand it was!— and a candlelight dinner and drank to the future and how their lives were going to change and then they got undressed and they made wonderful love. And then they were lying there afterwards, my mother told me, and they both kind of stiffened, and panic set in. And they turned to each other and said, you know—oh God, what are we doing? We're not ready for this! We can't be parents yet!''

Rafi was chuckling lightly beside her.

"So they agreed the time wasn't really quite right and they should wait and think about it a bit longer before taking any further steps."

"How human your parents sound. So how did you manage, given such a hurdle?"

She smiled. "Well, it was already too late. I was already there."

"Excellent." He nuzzled her neck gently. "I am glad you were so quick to see your window of opportunity. How would I have managed the rest of my life if you had been stargazing at that moment?"

His certainty was so enticing. Zara fell silent with wishing.

After a few moments he prompted her. "So you proved from the start to be a determined soul."

"That's what my mother always said. Whenever I was difficult as a child, she would say, 'Don't you blame me! No one forced you to come here! You wanted to come, too!'"

He lay back laughing. "What an extraordinary woman she must be! Maddy." He tasted the name. "I'm looking forward to meeting her."

His confidence was infectious. When he spoke like that, as if all this were going to pass and their lives return to normal…as if it was a foregone conclusion that they would overcome everything and get married…her heart was always lighter. Zara laughed too.

"What is it?"

"Oh, just the thought of my mother's face when I tell her the Prince of East Barakat wants to meet her," Zara explained lamely.

"But you are an extraordinary woman. Your mother has

known all her life that you will do remarkable things, hasn't she? Why should it surprise her that a prince should fall in love with you?''

That seemed unanswerable, so she asked him what he had done while absent from the room that day.

''I searched for the entrance to the tunnel,'' he said.

She clutched him. ''You—you *searched?* What—how?''

''Do not fear for me, Zara,'' he said. ''I am a man blessed by fortune, it has always been so. Today I observed the site from within this fortress. I am working to create passages for myself through the parts of it that are abandoned and empty. Already I can move through five or six rooms that way—'' He indicated the hole into the next room. ''The building is built in a square around a very large courtyard, a typical pattern for many centuries here. Most of the citizens seem to live not in the fortress, but in simple structures in the courtyard. It is a communal life.

''I am sure that there is no entrance to the tunnel within the courtyard. That means it is either within the ruins or outside the fortress altogether. Do you remember anything that would give us a clue?''

She remembered the downhill travel, and the uphill, she remembered the dampness leaving the air…but how long had it been before she heard the voices, saw the light?

''It wasn't very long after we came up that I was lifted down from his horse…but would they build a tunnel to open right inside the fortress? Wouldn't that be risky?''

''I agree, but do you think it perhaps depends on the period when these things were built?''

She saw immediately what he meant. ''Yes, of course— whether they knew the tunnel opening was there when they built the fortress or whether it had already been buried. In that case it would be sheer chance that they chose this site. Otherwise—''

''What do you think the period of building might be?''

He was appealing to her expert knowledge. She had examined what she could of the walls, but without a larger view of the place it was extremely difficult.

"You told me the tunnel was attributed to Queen Halimah," Zara began.

He nodded. "I did, and it is, but many old structures are attributed to her which could not possibly be her work. She is renowned in our history for her public works, and naturally in centuries gone by, when people stumbled upon some forgotten bridge or building, they believed it was her doing. But it is not necessarily always the case."

"So the tunnel could be any age?"

"We know nothing about the tunnel except what you have experienced of it, and the brief historical mention that guesses it was built by my ancestress. In the time of that writer it was already old and fallen into disuse. Ibn Qalam wrote in the seventeenth century."

"And what about this fortress?"

He shrugged and smiled. "Archaeology is not one of my subjects. At the Sorbonne, I studied politics and statecraft. Not very useful in any occupation."

Zara was momentarily sidetracked. "You were at the Sorbonne?"

"I was, for my undergraduate degree."

"I did my Year Abroad at the Sorbonne! When were you there?"

Of course they had missed each other by several years, but suddenly Prince Rafi did not seem so much a stranger. She had imagined him a man locked completely within his own culture, with no understanding of her background except perhaps through his stepmother...but Zara began to think that she herself was far more culture-bound than he was.

"You speak French, too, then?"

"I do. Why does this surprise you?"

"Oh—it's just—I wish I spoke Arabic. But I've only got about five words."

"You said *Salaam aleikum* very beautifully in the morn-

The Editor's "Thank You" Free Gifts Include:

- Two BRAND-NEW romance novels!
- An exciting mystery gift!

PLACE
FREE GIFT
SEAL
HERE

YES!

I have placed my Editor's "Thank You" seal in the space provided above. Please send me 2 free books and a fabulous mystery gift. I understand I am under no obligation to purchase any books, as explained on the back and on the opposite page.

326 SDL CQUT

225 SDL CQUH
(S-D-06/99)

Name:

PLEASE PRINT

Address:

Apt.#:

City:

State/
Prov.:

Postal
Zip/Code:

Thank You!

The Silhouette Reader Service™ — Here's how it works:

Accepting your 2 free books and mystery gift places you under no obligation to buy anything. You may keep the books and gift and return the shipping statement marked "cancel." If you do not cancel, about a month later we'll send you 6 additional novels and bill you just $3.12 each in the U.S., or $3.49 each in Canada, plus 25¢ delivery per book and applicable taxes if any.* That's the complete price and — compared to the cover price of $3.75 in the U.S. and $4.25 in Canada — it's quite a bargain! You may cancel at any time, but if you choose to continue, every month we'll send you 6 more books, which you may either purchase at the discount price or return to us and cancel your subscription.

*Terms and prices subject to change without notice. Sales tax applicable in N.Y. Canadian residents will be charged applicable provincial taxes and GST.

If offer card is missing write to: The Silhouette Reader Service, 3010 Walden Ave., P.O. Box 1867, Buffalo, NY 14240-1867

BUSINESS REPLY MAIL
FIRST-CLASS MAIL   PERMIT NO. 717   BUFFALO, NY

POSTAGE WILL BE PAID BY ADDRESSEE

SILHOUETTE READER SERVICE
3010 WALDEN AVE
PO BOX 1867
BUFFALO NY 14240-9952

NO POSTAGE
NECESSARY
IF MAILED
IN THE
UNITED STATES

ing at the wadi. And you will learn the rest,'' Rafi said. ''You will have private tutors, and we will by no means always speak English to each other.''

She bit her lip. ''Rafi, you keep talking as if—'' She broke off.

''As if?'' he prompted.

''Well, as if I've agreed to—''

''To marry me? Yes, I speak like this, Beloved. But I will not press you so long as we remain here. I know you can give me no answer now. But I believe, I know that when this is over, and you breathe the air of freedom, you will come on a visit to me…then, then I will convince you. I will make you love me. You will see.''

She could not argue with that. At the moment she felt so confused, her thinking so disturbed by her imprisonment, that she could hardly imagine getting back her stability again. She found it difficult to imagine her release. Even after a few days her horizons seemed to have shrunk to these four pathetic walls.

They talked again, about her childhood. Rafi pressed her for detail, the sort of minute detail with which she had never previously examined her life. He wanted to know friends' names, and what clothes she had been wearing during an incident she was describing, and whether she liked her playmates' mothers or the teachers she named.

Zara stretched her mind, trying to remember, and suddenly, after a long time, something changed—she was *seeing* it. Her life was there before her in the darkened room. It was no longer an effort. She remembered details she hadn't thought of since the day they happened.

It had been a pretty conventional life, and yet, like every life, it was a tapestry. She began to see and understand things she had not seen before, to make connections between elements that had before seemed unconnected.

To find the pattern in the tapestry.

''I haven't thought of that for years!'' she would exclaim, remembering an incident that she now could see as in some way character forming. Her grandfather's interest in history—she had forgotten those visits to his study as a very young child, shortly before he died, where he would tell her stories about the ancient world.

"He was a writer, he wrote fiction about ancient Greece and things like that—he had been in a wheelchair ever since the war. I'm sure he told me once that he would have liked to go out to the ground where history had happened rather than get it all from books. I don't think I knew then that he was talking about an actual occupation…but he meant he'd have liked to be an archaeologist. He must have! And here I am…"

Rafi listened closely, he questioned gently, he was silent when she was silent in thought…she had never been given such deep attention in her life. She had never met anyone who was such a good listener.

He left when she began to fall asleep. The last thing she remembered was his kiss on her forehead, and then she was dreaming.

She dreamed she was falling in love with Rafi.

The next day the genie brought her a small metal file from his cache of magic. Zara, thrilled, excited, grateful almost to the point of tears, immediately set to work on the heavy padlock that held the chain that bound her. But they quickly discovered that it made a distinctive, carrying, high-pitched noise which Rafi could hear at a distance of several rooms.

"It will be safe to work on it for only a few minutes at a time," Rafi advised thoughtfully. "And in case someone comes, we must find a good hiding place for it within your reach. It will be risky. Do you want to do it?"

She couldn't bear inactivity when there was something she could be doing to gain her freedom. "Yes," she said. "Anyway, what's the point of finding the tunnel if I can't go out through it?"

"We will bring men through it to attack," he said. But

it was true that it would be a great deal safer to free Zara first, and she would weather imprisonment better if she were actively aiding her own escape through the tedious days.

They examined the stones near her by the light of his candle, and found a narrow crack not far from where her chain was embedded, in the seam where the wall met the floor. It was quite long, and wide enough to take the file. It wasn't very deep, either, she discovered by gingerly poking around with it, but she could slide the file in on a slant and it was almost perfectly hidden.

They agreed she would work on the padlock for a few minutes twice each day, after the old woman had visited her, to reduce the risk of someone coming on her unexpectedly.

Zara suddenly felt real again. She was human. She could do things that mattered.

That afternoon, when he came to bring some purloined fruit for her lunch, the genie brought her another pail of water, and she had another sponge bath and washed her hair.

As she sat combing it out, feeling blissfully cool and clean, Rafi said, "I have to try to get a message to my brothers soon. I will do it under cover of darkness. You will be here alone. You should have light if possible. I know you will worry until I return. But I am afraid someone will see the light and come to investigate."

"Oh," Zara said in a small voice, because he was right. Waiting would be far easier if she had a candle. Darkness made her feel so helpless, but they had agreed that the candle should be used only in emergencies.

"Perhaps if you ask the old woman for a candle when she comes next, she will take pity on you."

"Oh! Yes, she might, Rafi, she seems very—concerned for me."

"I will teach you the Arabic for candle. It is *shama'a*."

"Shama'a," Zara said. When he nodded she repeated it two or three times.

He smiled that smile of approval that always melted her. "You see how quickly you will learn to speak to my people," he said. "It is a beautiful language, too, that you will enjoy learning—intricate and precise."

"Precise," she repeated smilingly. "Yes, I've heard there are about twenty words for *camel.*"

"And do not you in English have as many words for *dog?*"

She lifted an eyebrow. "We do? Pooch and dog, that's all I know."

"And hound, bitch, pup, cur, mutt, canine, mongrel. And also shepherd, terrier, basset, beagle…dozens of breed names. Am I not right?"

"Oh," was all she could say to that. Sometimes she felt as if every time he opened his mouth, Rafi gave her some new experience, showed her some barrier in her thinking. She was being stretched in a way that she had not felt at university. There everything she learned somehow fit into her already known image of the world, or broadened it only in easy, predictable ways. Rafi was constantly showing her things that did not fit, so that she had to change her image— or step outside it—to accommodate them.

Soon it was close to the time that the old woman might be expected. Rafi wanted to use the last of the sunlight in any case, for his explorations. At night he used a flashlight, but there was danger in that.

When she was left alone, Zara fretted. Now that there was something productive she could do, she was desperate for the old woman to come and go so that she could begin on the padlock.

So eager was she, she almost forgot about asking for the candle. It wasn't till the old woman returned for the second time with her empty pail that she smiled and said pleadingly, *"Shama'a?"*

"Ahhh!" exclaimed the old woman, with a jumble of

words that Zara knew expressed surprise at her coming up with the word. A short speech followed, accompanied by a clap of her hands and a pitying tone of voice that seemed to be saying no, it would not be possible. *He* would refuse.

She didn't let the old woman finish. *"Shama'a?"* she begged again.

Between sign language and murmurs the old woman signalled—but a light! What was the good of a candle without something to light it with?

Zara's heart sank. Why hadn't they thought of this? Oh, what fools they were! She could have kept Rafi's lighter and shown it—how would the woman guess that it had not been in her pocket from the start? But now...

She lifted her hands in resignation and smiled woefully, giving in to the old woman's argument.

The old woman leaned down, her wrinkled brown hand stretching to Zara's cheek, and muttered again. *Poor child! Poor child!* her tone suggested. With a lingering, sorrowful glance, she went out.

Fighting impatience, Zara counted to a hundred, then made a dive for her precious metal file. She began the ritual they had agreed upon—filing hard for a few seconds, and then a pause to listen. Filing again. Rub dirt into the shiny wound she was making in the metal, so that it would be less noticeable if anyone checked. She could keep it up for no more than a few minutes.

Impatient as she was, Zara knew how important it was to be careful. It would be worse than foolish to risk the whole enterprise by being over-eager now. So she filed, listened, rubbed, filed.

It was while she was rubbing dirt onto the metal for what she had decided was the last time that she suddenly heard the sounds of someone approaching in the passageway. Sitting straight with a start, Zara snatched up the file and slipped it hastily into the little crack they had found for it.

She was a little too hasty. Or maybe they should have checked out the hole more thoroughly. Because instead of finding its previous resting place on stone, the file slipped from her fingers. She heard the unmistakable sound of it falling flat on the stones under the floor, several inches out of the reach of her fingers.

Ten

It was the old woman, coming jubilantly and triumphantly in, holding aloft a candle and a cigarette lighter in either hand. Zara was biting her lip against tears—but she knew she had to react with gratitude to what was evidently a coup.

"Thank you, *shokran jazilan!*" she murmured over and over, as the old woman squatted down beside her and showed her the wonderful technology by which the cheap plastic lighter worked. There was only a tiny amount of fuel left in it, Zara saw. She wondered whether Jalal had given permission, or whether the old woman had done this in secret.

"*Shokran jazilan!*" she kept saying, bending her head to hide her distress. "*Shokran, shokran!*"

The old woman put her hand under Zara's chin and lifted it. Tears she could not control slipped down her cheeks. "Aiiiii!" wailed the woman on a long falling note. She

wiped the tears with a gentle, work-roughened forefinger,
and murmured cajolingly.

She thought Zara was crying in gratitude for the candle.
Zara smiled and blinked back the tears as the woman consoled her. *It's all right, poor little one. There, there. It's
all right.*

She allowed herself to be consoled. But when the old
woman had left her alone again, she lit the candle with
trembling urgency, impatiently brushed away her tears and
tried to see down the crack where the file had fallen.

Her fingers would not go in past the knuckle, and she
could feel nothing but air. Zara tried to pry away bits of
mortar with her fingers, but considering what a ruin she
was inhabiting, it was infuriatingly firm.

The candle was short. She knew Rafi had more, but still
it was stupid to waste it. So she gave up on the hopeless
task and lay down, watching the sun set by means of the
diminishing light in the passage, waiting for Rafi to return.
She hoped he would come back after his search and before
he tried to get the message to his brothers. Surely he
wouldn't make any attempt till the camp was settled for
the night? It would be a long wait if he did not come....

She was already deeply dependent on him. Her emotions
were volatile and far too near the surface now, and Rafi
was her refuge and her strength. She felt a deep need of
him, a yearning for him…but she wasn't herself. She didn't
need a master's in psychology to understand that the powerful feelings she had for him might be the result of her
isolation.

Yet she felt that her dream was true, that she was falling
deeply in love with him, that he was the one she had been
waiting for, that whenever and wherever she had met him,
she would have felt it.

When she had first met him, she had thought him a bandit, and even then she had felt the pull, argued this side of
her. Surely that showed that they were, as Rafi insisted,
naturally drawn to each other?

She began to dream a little. If she did not love him, it would be a terrible mistake to marry him, she knew. To come to a strange country for the rest of her life, to make such a huge change—to take on the massive responsibility of being queen to a people—all that would be intolerable without a deep and abiding bond.

If she *did* love him, she was sure he would be a wonderful husband. He was brave, he was honourable, with a nobility of nature as well as being noble by birth. He was so thoughtful of her, so protective, and he listened to her in a way she wasn't used to. She was sure that wasn't common. And he had such a rich imagination, and a sense of humour…how could any woman choose better?

Zara thought of the ring, and drew it to her lips in the fading light. It caught a last glimmer from somewhere, and sparkled once, like a beacon of promise. Just before sleep she kissed it, rubbing it with her lips, and wished…

They came to her as she lay in her high white bed between silken sheets. *His Highness desires her presence,* she heard them whisper. *He commands it.*

We hear and obey, said other voices.

She felt their hands on her skin as she slept, delicate, gently lifting the silken sheets and drawing them back, carefully lifting her body. She awoke then. *What is it?* she asked drowsily.

Madame, he has asked for thee. He awaits thee. We are come to take thee to the baths.

A shiver of delight ran through her body. *He has asked for me?*

In her was the knowledge that she was newly entered to the harem, that she had arrived only today, and when the Sultan of All the Worlds had accepted her as a gift, he had cast an interested eye over her veiled form as she stepped from the litter that brought her and made her obeisance in the huge Throne Room…

He has, Madame. The bath is ready.

They led her through a bewildering series of rooms and
then through a door and into the great *hamam*. In the centre
the male slaves, their powerfully muscled arms and strong
chests gleaming with oil, awaited her.

They surrounded her and carefully began to disrobe her.
Her clothes were white, and they stripped off layer after
layer until she was naked under their admiring gaze. She
saw them exchange glances under lowered eyelids.

He will be pleased with thee, Mistress, they said.

She only smiled, and allowed herself to be led down into
the warm water.

She dived and swam deep. On the walls and floor of the
bath were images of men and women that made her gasp.
She found that she could breathe underwater, and stayed
there, watching the images.

They seemed to move with the flow of the water past
her eyes. Handsome black-eyed men, beautiful women with
hair like her own, long, flowing curls…they kissed and
toyed with each other, and smiled and flicked lazy glances
of desire.

She felt heat in her belly, and thought of the Sultan of
All the Worlds, who had summoned her the very night of
her arrival, and the heat increased.

They bathed her with soaps of a most delicious softness,
like cream on her creamy skin. They washed her hair, and
rinsed her carefully, and they drew her from the bath.

She lay on a bed of velvet, and a thousand hands massaged and stroked her. Perfume was rubbed deep into her
skin, so that she became the perfume. The heat in her belly
moved to her loins, and then to all parts of her—skin, hair,
lips, eyes—under their caresses, and she thought of nothing
but the man for whom they prepared her, and what he
would demand of her, and how willingly she would give
it.

She could not remember his face, for she had scarcely
dared to glance up at it, but he had excited her. Thrilled
her. His voice when he whispered to a courtier his approval;

his hand as he negligently signalled that she should be taken to the harem…she had melted with desire for him even then, and had wondered how long before he thought of her again. Whether he would ever think of her, ever send for her…

The slaves stroked every part of her, scenting her skin, making her a perfect offering to the one who was called the Sultan of All the Worlds. With careful assiduity and melting softness, they tinted her skin with palest cream. They outlined her eyes with blackest black, and her finger-tips and toes with a deeper pink. Then they dyed her lips, her nipples—and even her tender, hidden bud—with sweetest pink.

They dressed her in cloth of silver. A tiny jacket that barely covered her breasts, so that the fullness of the two globes just showed beneath. A pair of trousers of thinnest gauze, full and flowing from below her waist to her feet, gathered in at her ankles. All her stomach and abdomen left naked.

Not only her stomach and abdomen. The pants were not stitched between her legs. The seam was open. *Show him this only at the last,* they advised her. *He will be well pleased with the trick. It is new.*

They argued about stones. *Ruby, emerald, sapphire,* murmured different voices. Ruby won. Ruby to match her lips, that had been red without the dye.

So they placed a large jewel in her navel, that glinted rose in the lights as she moved. They placed jewels also in her ears, her nose, on her fingers and toes, and sprinkled through the curls of her hair. They locked a jewelled belt to sway around her hips.

They stood back to admire. *Beautiful,* they agreed, with soft whispers. *Lady, you will be fortunate. When you are elevated to position, remember us, who helped you there.*

She promised. *Each of you shall have one petition answered if it is as you say,* she vowed.

They draped a cloth of ruby-spangled silver over her hair and face. *Now,* they said.

Another door opened. They led her through rooms and halls of steadily increasing beauty and magnificence. She heard music from a distance. Gold and jewels glinted from the walls. Lamps glowed behind carved wooden screens, casting magic shadows. She was terrified and thrilled together. The music played in the same rhythm as her pounding heartbeat, building long and slow to a distant but inevitable crescendo.

And then she was there, in the Sultan's own private rooms. The hangings were lushly ornate. There were paintings of men and women in intimate embrace on the walls, that sent shivers of desire through her. There was light and shadow and perfume and incense.

She was melting. They opened the one she knew was the last door, and then she entered alone. The room was dark, shadowed, huge. Through a high arched window, far away, she saw the full moon and the stars in a midnight sky. Beside it, at the far end of the room, was a bed, draped with beautiful cloths.

She knew that he was there, on the bed.

At a signal, the music started again. Seductive, demanding music.

She saw a pale hand in the shadows of the bed.

Dance for me, said a voice. His voice.

The music already urged her to dance. Her arms rose of their own accord, and she understood that she was a dancer of great skill. She began to move, with the tiniest movements of her hips, her face still hidden from him.

The floor was cool under her feet. They were the only part of her not afire with desire, with wishing. Her hips increased their movement, her arms swaying like dancing serpents in accompaniment. The jewel in her navel glinted and glowed with each flexion of perfect muscle. Those in her ears, her nose, on her fingers and toes, and in her jewelled belt sent wild shafts of coloured light all around the walls.

She danced, and each step, each movement made her more faint, more intoxicated. She smiled behind the silvery veil that still hid her face from him, and as the dance went on she began to toy with the veil, and with the promise of unveiling her face and hair for his delectation.

She sensed his attention. She had caught him—he wanted to see what woman was in that lush body, behind that spangled gauze. She dropped it first to show her eyes, holding the gauzy fabric still in front of her lower face, and sent dark glances of passion towards the shadows of the bed.

At last, as the music reached a crescendo, she whirled and spun, and lifted the veil above her head to trail behind her in the air. She heard the intake of breath from the shadows of the bed and stopped as the music stopped.

Then there was silence.

Approach, said the beloved voice.

Fearlessly, and yet full of trepidation, she stepped forward till she stood at the end of the huge, canopied bed. Still he was in shadow.

Come further, he commanded, and she entered the shadows to be with him.

They were in a world apart, the world of shadows. He was bare chested, barefoot, wearing gold trousers, and wore a gold turban with a rich green jewel.

He held a glass of intoxicating liquid, which he offered to her. There were sweetmeats. At his bidding, she ate and drank, and her wild intoxication increased.

Still she did not see his face. He ate, and placed tender morsels of food between her lips. They struck her tongue with shooting flavours that seemed to enter her being. *Delicious,* she said gratefully.

Yes, said he, but he meant—her.

At last, at long awaited last, his hands were upon her.

She felt his touch on the underside of her exposed breast, and murmured softly of hunger.

His fingers found her breast, the nipple. He stroked it while her throat helplessly moaned its quiet delirium. *You see how it will be,* he told her. *You love me without knowing it.*

Yes, she said. *I knew it when I saw you.* The fire in her was already wilder than anything she had ever felt. Her limbs burned with icy hot hunger for his touch. He stroked her—breasts, stomach, abdomen.

They know how to please me, he said, *and yet I have never been so pleased with a woman.*

Nor I, with a Sultan, she murmured, and he laughed.

Only then did she understand her danger. If he had not laughed…

But he had no choice. His touch drugged her, and drugged him. They were made for each other's delight. *Give me your lips,* he said.

She offered up the pink-dyed flesh, and he devoured it. His tongue entered her mouth, inviting her to do the same in return, and then when she did, he gnawed at it with hungry intensity.

His hand strayed along her arms, over her abdomen. *Are you a Peri, that you affect me so?* he asked.

She only smiled, and he thought that it was true. *This…how is this fastened?* he asked, of the silver cloth that hid her breasts from his eyes and mouth.

So, she said with a smile, opening the fastenings for him. Her breasts were revealed, white and pink, and his shadowed eyes were frighteningly black with interest. *I tell thee, there has never been a woman like thee,* he said.

His hands touched and stroked her full breasts, and she moaned. *There has never been a woman I would please so,* he said. *Give me your rosebud lips.*

They kissed. Her heart sang, her body shook with pleasure. His hand moved hungrily between her legs, and then he found the secret.

What is this? he demanded, one hand with firm command spreading her legs for his gaze as she lay on soft pillows. Obediently she spread her legs, and then the treasure was revealed. His breath hissed between his teeth.

What jewel is this? he asked, the silver cloth parting to reveal the pink-dyed hungry bud. *No, not jewel, but delicious fruit.*

His dark head bent over her, and she felt the burning, spiralling heat of his tongue where the silver cloth granted him access. *No woman has ever moved me like this,* he breathed, and of its own accord, her body arched and jerked with the pleasure of his hot breath, his heated tongue. *Again,* he said, and his face lowered between her thighs.

She exploded then, melting with heat and sweetness. She cried with a deep, primitive, hunger-sated, still-hungry voice, and he felt the wildness sweep through him.

Who art thou? he demanded.

I love you, she said, and of its own accord, her hand reached for him, for the hard, hungry centre of his being, for the ramrod sex that her body demanded should make part of her own being.

Is it so? he cried. *Then open thyself to me, for I am hungered with thee.*

She spread her legs. He rose up above her, strong and hard yet melting gold, over her body of white and pink and silver. He thrust into her, between the folds of spangled silver, into the path of pink, and she gasped with the sensation that flowed through her.

"Rafi!" she cried then, seeing his face for the first time.

"Zara!" he replied. He tried to say more, but he was swept with feeling, and with the need to thrust and pound his way inside the cavern of his yearning.

Zara felt total confusion, mingled with the most delicious sensations she had ever experienced. Her body shook with simultaneous hunger and fulfilment.

"Rafi!" she cried again. "What is it?"

It is love, said the Sultan of All the Worlds.

And she shook and trembled with the pleasure he gave
her, and knew that it was so.

Rafi returned very late. He had had great difficulty in
signalling. Jalal's guards were too watchful.

"They have a military precision, though they look like
a bunch of ruffians," he told Zara. "They murmur the pass-
word very quietly. I heard it last time, but tonight I could
not get close enough and had to wait. My brothers have
news."

"What?" she asked excitedly. She had been sleeping,
but had woken up when he merely put his head through
the hole in the wall. Now they sat by candlelight, talking
softly.

"We will find out tomorrow. Tomorrow the foodstuffs
are due for delivery again by Mustafa. One of my Companions will come in with him in place of his brother. We
agreed on this as a fail-safe."

They were leaning against the wall, side by side. Zara
yawned, and Rafi put his arm around her and pulled her to
rest on his shoulder.

"It is late. I did not mean to wake you. Lie down now
and get some sleep."

"I'm glad I woke up. I'm not really sleepy now. I have
to tell you what I did with the file," she said, and then
sadly confessed.

He listened to the tale of woe, and her self-blame for not
having asked the old woman for a candle on her first trip,
and on several other points.

"Don't you think we could get it out again if we had a
stick with something sticky on the end of it?" she finished.

Then he smiled and said, "Do not grieve over this thing.
If it is God's will, we will find a way to retrieve the file.
But let us wait until tomorrow. Let me speak to my Com-
panion and learn what my brothers are planning."

She had done her crying; it wasn't hard to do as he said.
"All right."

They sat in silence, and she thought of her dreams, and of what it meant to learn that she loved him, and feel the truth of it. Unconsciously she sighed.

He was always quick to sense her feelings. "Tell me, Beloved," he said.

"I'll have a lot to learn if I marry you, won't I?"

"Does it frighten you?"

"Yes, a little. I'd be a fool if it didn't, wouldn't I?"

He was silent, his black eyes grave. His hold tightened around her. "We are young, Zara. You are twenty-five, I am thirty. Whatever happens to us, we have a lot to learn. You are not a woman who will give up learning new things. The question is not *whether,* but *what* we choose to learn. Whether you marry me or not, the future is full of new things, of surprises, of truths, of experiences that you have so far not dreamed of. You are a woman who travels far in the search of knowledge. You will never in any case settle down—will you?—and be pleased to think that you know it all.

"The culture of my people will be no more difficult for you to learn than the ancient world of Alexander. It will, even, be easier. Whereas now you seek answers from stone, I will be there at every step to answer your questions. And I assure you, I am not at all like stone. When you ask me questions, I will answer. Just as, when you touch me, my blood will always run."

Eleven

When her ray of sun awoke them the next morning they were still wrapped in each other's arms. Rafi yawned and kissed her lightly. "Is this not pleasant, to wake up with each other? Does it feel to you like something you can spend the rest of your life doing?"

But before she could answer, he abruptly remembered where they were. He smothered an exclamation and murmured, "I should not have fallen asleep here. The old woman or Jalal might have come in—it will be very dangerous for both of us if my presence is discovered."

He left her soon afterwards, because during the morning bustle of the encampment he could risk walking around without too much danger. Everyone came and went, and he was just another figure in a white keffiyeh.

Zara performed her morning rituals when he was gone. She always had enough water to drink now, for there was a well in the courtyard and Rafi had managed to steal a pail which he kept next door, full of water. So she could rinse her face and hands and brush her teeth every morning, and comb the dust out of her hair with a wet comb.

Then she sat down to wait. This was the hardest part now of her imprisonment—the sheer mind-numbing boredom of having nothing to do. She had not wished on the ring for a book to read or a deck of cards, but she certainly did wish she had something to keep her mind occupied. It was too easy to slip into fear and negative thinking.

But she could at least think about her dream. She spent an hour seeing it all again, the palace ruins, the slaves, her costumes...the eyes of the Sultan of All the Worlds.

She thought, too, about what Rafi had said about waking up beside him. It was true—her heart had been singing when she awoke to find him there. It had a feeling of rightness. He did not seem a relative stranger, but someone she knew well...and would come to know better.

When he returned, slipping through the wall, he was muttering softly, "Ow, ow, ow!" and making a curious mewling sound. Zara leapt to her feet, her heart racing.

"Rafi, what is it?" she hissed hoarsely. "What's wrong?"

His shirt was bulging strangely on one side of his waist, and he had his hand clutched there. Through her mind flashed the image of a gunshot wound and a makeshift bandage. But the bandage seemed to be moving quite vigorously. Zara stared in confusion.

"Your genie returns, lady!" Rafi cried. "And none too soon—I might have screamed and given myself away! *Ow,* you little monster, don't you know when you have a benefactor?" he demanded, grabbing at the bulge in his shirt and pulling it away from him. With the other he was unbuttoning the shirt. He reached gingerly in.

His hand came out full of writhing fur, claws and whiskers. And a little pink mouth that mewed its fury at him.

"A *kitten!*" Zara cried. "Oh, Rafi! How did you—"

"Careful!" he warned her. "It's got claws like needles."

She was laughing almost uncontrollably. Rafi held the

tiny little creature in one hand, well away, and all four paws were wildly clawing, trying to get to his hand. It was an image of David and Goliath—the desert warrior defeated by a few ounces of grey and white fur.

"Go ahead and laugh," he said plaintively. He set the kitten down on the floor, where it immediately scampered to a fold of her blanket and crept under. Rafi eyed it balefully as he began to pull at his shirt. "I'll have to wash the blood off me, because I will become identifiable if I have a bloodstained shirt. I thought kittens were supposed to be gentle things. Who started that myth, or is this one just a monster?"

"Well, naturally she thinks you're a danger," Zara explained placatingly. "How is she to know your noble nature when you haven't been properly introduced?"

"She seems to know yours."

The kitten had turned around under the fold of blanket and was now blinking out at the world. Zara, crouching before her, carefully extended a finger, and the kitten sniffed it curiously.

"She's got a very pretty face. Where did you find her?"

"There are half a dozen who hang around the communal cooking area, waiting for the scraps that the women throw them. They all seem to be from one litter, and I didn't think anyone would notice if one went missing. If it's found here of course you can pretend it wandered in."

He took his shirt off, and Zara stood to examine his battle wounds. They were surprisingly extensive. Not deep, but there was a network of tiny lines all around one half of his waist and lower chest, along which blood was starting to seep in little teardrops. "Goodness, how long was she inside your shirt?"

"Only a few minutes. Another minute and I'd have had to release her, though," he joked.

Zara nodded, feeling suddenly sober. "Maybe that's what I should have done to Jalal. Bitten and scratched till he let me go."

He put his hand on her cheek, his eyes serious. "It would have been very dangerous. You were on a galloping horse, and he was in no mood to relinquish a hostage so valuable. You might have been badly hurt, if not killed."

The blood was starting to drip now. "I have no cloth or anything!" Zara said. "I'll just have to wipe it off with water and my bare hands."

She damped her hands by pouring a little water from her drinking pot over them, then ran them over his side and stomach, two or three times, rinsing off the blood. His body was very firm with muscle, his chest broad and covered with dark curling hair, his waist narrow, his arms strong…with her hands flat against his flesh, Zara paused, and the touch between them was suddenly electric.

She was afraid to look up into his face. She stood frozen there, while sensation zinged from her fingertips and palms and shot trembling along her arms and into her body.

Too late, she lifted her hands away from that dangerous touch. But the electricity did not stop when the connection was broken. Rafi lifted his hands and, her head bent, she saw how those strong but elegant fingers grasped her upper arms. "Zara," he whispered hoarsely.

She raised her head, expecting his kiss. Wanting it. Not wanting to think about what it meant, but only wanting that full, strong mouth, the taste of it on her tongue.

He said, "Zara, if I touch you the way I want to touch you now, I will lose control. It is not safe here. I want to kiss you, I want…but if I do, it will not, it cannot stop with a kiss. I know myself, I know you…I know how much I want from you and want to give you. I have never felt desire like this for any woman. If I make love to you, I will—I have known it from the moment I saw you at the waterfall—I will be lost.

"So I will not kiss you now, Zara. Not when there is such desire between us. When my brothers and I have taken you safely out of your prison, then…then." He nodded. "I tell you this because a woman likes to know that a man

desires as well as loves her. But I must hide my desire both
from you and from myself, so long as we are in this place.''

Her blood was champagne. The bubbles ran through her
system, making her light with joyous laughter and aching
desire. Never had any man's expressed desire so enchanted
her, so thrilled her. Her blood rushed to and fro in her, for
the sheer joy of the exercise.

''All right,'' she said, an irrepressible smile teasing her
mouth. She wondered when a man had ever before in her
experience put his own sexual need second to her needs.
Never, probably. Sexual desire and selfishness, in her experience, seemed to go together.

A woman didn't have to be in prison to appreciate such
a man. Any woman in the world, she thought, would love
him.

The kitten did not at all like being bathed, but Zara had
no intention of adding fleas to her expanding family. So it
was soaped and rinsed thoroughly in the pail of water, and
then dried—on a square torn from Zara's once-beautiful
white silk dress, whose existence she had suddenly remembered. Then, notwithstanding the tiny claws, she sat down
and by the light of Rafi's flashlight—which it seemed safe
to use during the day—ruthlessly checked the kitten for
fleas.

A little surprisingly, she did not find any. Zara set the
still-indignant kitten down on a fresh square of the white
silk, where it immediately began to groom itself.

Rafi, meanwhile, had gone, after removing all evidence
of the kitten's ablutions except for the flashlight. He also
left behind a few morsels of meat which he had picked up
along with the cat.

When the kitten was fully recovered, Zara amused herself by feeding it the little tidbits of meat. It ate greedily.
It was thin, but not starving, and now that the dust of the
place had been thoroughly cleaned from its fur, it looked
as healthy as any other kitten. It was very pretty and con-

fiding, and quickly forgave and forgot the bathing episode. It explored the little cell, but one hiss from Zara was enough to convince it not to go out into the passage. Then it returned to the little square of white on her bed, settled itself against her thigh, licked a paw, and promptly fell asleep.

Zara didn't think that she had ever in her life been so delighted with the company of a fellow creature. Just watching the kitten sleep made her heart lighter.

The flashlight was still beside her. Rafi had left while she was examining the kitten, reminding her to hide the light if the old woman came in his absence. Zara began tucking it out of sight under the blanket, when a thought crossed her mind, and instead she knelt down beside the crack in the floor where the file had fallen and shone the light into the aperture.

It was the kitten who saved her. Zara heard an exclamation from the passage and surfaced with shock to realize that she had been trying to see down into the hole for minutes, totally lost to her surroundings. Meanwhile, the kitten had awakened refreshed and had ventured into the passage at a critical moment. When the kitten and the old woman spied each other, the old woman cried out, and the kitten made a dash for the haven of Zara's bed.

Zara had time only to bury the flashlight under her blanket, turn her ring in towards her palm, a move that was second nature to her now, and sit on the exposed edge of her mattress before the old woman came in exclaiming.

Now how did the kitten find its way in here?

"Mash'allah," Zara responded. *It must have been God's will.*

God looks after his little ones. Here, my little one, here is food and drink for you.

Zara accepted the flat bread rolled around a succulent piece of meat with noises of gratitude. She did not often get meat, and she missed it. But she bit a tiny piece off first and offered it to the fascinated kitten.

Ya Allah! You don't mean to feed the animal from your own mouth?

But it is my friend. I cannot let it starve.

The old woman shook her head. *I will bring you a little food for it. Do not give it your own, you are too hungry.* How easy it was to communicate ideas around such a subject as a kitten. The mixture of sign language, body language and vocal outbursts was clear to each.

And a little bowl for water, Zara begged.

Nodding, cackling, delighted with their ability to communicate, the old woman poured out water for Zara, picked up the latrine and left. *I'll come right back.*

She returned a few minutes later with a broken saucer and a little gristly meat and fat. The sight of this made Zara understand how carefully the old woman had chosen the delectable meat in her own sandwich. She watched as the old woman bent down to stroke the kitten's head, then patted Zara's cheek.

The kitten is as pretty as you. Jalal says Prince Rafi loves you. You are so lovely, it is no surprise.

When the old woman left, Zara played with the kitten, waiting for Rafi's return. She tore a strip from the piece of white silk she had used to make its bed, and laughed at its antics trying to catch the strip, able to forget herself and where she was more completely than she could have imagined possible a few days ago.

When Rafi returned at last, she was lying on her back, the kitten standing on her chest pawing at her lips as she blew air and made little noises, laughing in helpless amusement in between.

He stood on the other side of the wall for a moment, watching in appreciation. Her beautiful hair was splayed out beneath her, her legs in a posture of graceful abandon, her attention entirely on the kitten. Just so might the favourite of the harem have toyed with a kitten, in decades and centuries past.

But the moment he stepped through the wall, she grabbed

the kitten and swung herself up to a sitting position and full attention. "Is everything all right?"

"It is very well." He was carrying a thin stick of what glowed, even behind a badly scratched surface, like marble. He sat down, laying this gently on the floor beside him.

"Did your Companion come in?"

"Arif has been here and is safely gone. He brought the message from my brother. They had much to tell me." Rafi smiled. "The first is that, thanks to your ingenuity, Zara, they have found the tunnel."

She squealed and choked the sound back, her hands flying to her mouth in happy astonishment. "They did? How?"

"At night, in helicopters. Your robe of honour reflected the spotlight. They marked the place and returned in the morning. Not fifty yards away from where your robe was lying, a pile of rocks like any other in the desert disguises the entrance. Jalal of course has no suspicion that we know of the existence of the tunnel. By great good fortune the outcrop is hidden from the view of this fortress by a much larger pile nearby, but they are being very careful nevertheless not to have any activity in the immediate area, in case he is surveilling them."

She was almost speechless with gratitude and relief. "Oh, oh thank God! Oh, Rafi, how wonderful! Have they come all the way through it? Does it lead into this camp?"

"The exploration must be done with great caution. Jalal must certainly have guards inside the tunnel—he would be a fool if he did not, and he is not a fool. We dare not signal to Jalal that it has been found—he might take…" Rafi broke off. "Take steps. He might even destroy the tunnel."

The archaeologist in her leapt to the surface. "Oh, God, don't let him do that! I want to explore it when this is over! It must be a fascinating piece of history."

He smiled at her enthusiasm. "Yes, let us hope we avoid destroying something that has lasted so long."

"What will your brothers do?"

"In three days there is a celebration here—it is an old custom among the desert tribes. I have heard conversations among the women about the feast. We will use the opportunity. I must locate the entrance to the tunnel at this side. If it is as we imagine, you can be taken through the tunnel to safety before the attack begins. That will be the safest way."

Her heart thumped with nervous anticipation.

"How will—how will it happen?"

He wrapped an arm around her. "Tonight," he said, "I will tell you another story from the Book of Kingly Wisdom. And then you will guess yourself, Beloved. It is one of the reasons why princes were encouraged to read such books. So that in difficult moments they might remember the tricks of their ancestors.

"But first we must see about retrieving the file. With this." Grinning, he reached into his pocket and pulled out a familiar-looking packet. It was white and printed with Arabic lettering in pink, but it was nevertheless unmistakable. It was open, but there were three or four sticks of gum in it. "Never again will I complain about my Companion Arif's gum-chewing propensities. He had this in his pocket."

Much later, Rafi returned from another exploration with some fruit, and a little meat for the kitten. The kitten ate ravenously and then fell asleep where it was, exhausted by its day of entertaining the prisoner.

Rafi, too, was exhausted. He had spent vain hours in another search for the tunnel. She could see he was a little dispirited by his failure. But her news would cheer him up. She let him settle and sink his teeth into a ripe piece of fruit, and then, like a conjuror, produced her exhibit.

Rafi sat up, astonished, the fruit forgotten, a grin splitting his face. "The file!" he exclaimed, wrapping his arms around her. "Zara! You did it!"

"Thank Mr. Wrigley, not me."

He sat back and gazed at her. "Who is Mr. Wrigley?"

"The man who invented chewing gum, I think!" she told him with a grin. They laughed.

"But this is excellent!" He picked up the stick of marble and examined the little pad of chewing gum still adhering to one end. "It took you a long time?"

She blew air up over her face. "Long enough." She nodded. "If I hadn't had the other Mr. Wriggly to amuse me in between I think I'd have screamed." Before he could ask, she said, "That's the kitten's new name. Mr. Wriggly."

Rafi grinned, and felt his disappointment over his own day lift in the presence of her good humour. They ate the fruit laughing and chatting, and flirting at each other with their eyes in a way that made their blood race pleasantly.

Then Zara declared, "It's time for my story now," and Rafi blew out the candle and they lay down together.

"Is this another story about King Mahmoud?" Zara asked.

"It is," Rafi explained. She realized how pleasant his voice was. She would probably enjoy a telephone book recital from him. "One day an old woman came to his Hall of Justice and complained because in a certain area of the kingdom, where she lived, they were troubled by a ruthless band of bandits."

"Oh!"

"Mahmoud asked her where this place was, and when she told him the name of it, he said, 'We don't really have much control over that region.' But the old woman said to him, 'I am a homeowner, and I control my house and garden. Are you a king, and you say do not have control over your own territory?'

"Mahmoud was shamed, and he asked her for details. She said that the bandits lived in a stronghold in the mountains and were very wild. They controlled all the caravan routes and regularly robbed the caravans and all the honest people who lived around. She herself had lost money and possessions to the bandits and she felt that as it was Mahmoud's fault for not keeping law and order, he ought to repay her.''

''Is this the same king whose courtiers were terrified because he had a hangover?'' Zara demanded.

He touched her nose. ''Ah, but a king must always let a subject speak unpleasant truths.''

''Must he?''

''Of course. Now, do not interrupt the story. Mahmoud promised the old woman that he would establish law in the area and wipe out the bandits. And he thought for awhile, and then he sent out a proclamation saying that a caravan protected by the king's troop would be going into that area, and all those who had business there could join it.

''There were many merchants who had feared to go into the area because of the bandits, and at this summons they all began to assemble. And before very long a hugely rich caravan was ready to set off.

''On the night before the departure, Mahmoud called one of his troop leaders to him, and gave him certain instructions. And the next day, the caravan set off. It was an enormous caravan, with hundreds of camels laden with all manner of the richest goods. It proceeded for days and weeks, and at last arrived in the area where the bandits held sway.

''And one day the residents of the place where they camped came out to them and told the merchants and the soldiers that a huge group of bandits was hiding at a certain point that the caravan would reach on the following day, ready to ambush the caravan.

''The merchants became very nervous at this, and some talked of turning back, but the leader of Mahmoud's men talked to them, saying that their lives would not be in danger because it was the soldiers' duty to take the risk to themselves. And he told them that Mahmoud had a plan that would wipe out the bandits, and that if they followed his instructions all would be well.

''So the merchants agreed to go on. Now among the

camels that made up Mahmoud's part of the caravan were ten camels loaded with apples. And that night, the Leader of the King's Troop had all the baskets of apples brought into his tent. Then he took out of his wallet the bottle of poison which King Mahmoud had given him, and a needle, and he carefully dipped the needle into the poison and then into each of the apples. Then he had the apples all loaded back onto the camels.

"The next morning, he called several of his men together and instructed them what to do. Then he said to the merchants, 'In a few hours we will reach the place where the robbers lie in ambush. When they attack, all the merchants should flee to safe ground. As for me and my men, we will put up a token resistance only. When you see me wheel my mount and gallop off, all of you follow me. We will regroup and in an hour will attack again.

"So they proceeded on to the ambush, and everyone did as instructed. The merchants fled as soon as the bandits came out of the bushes, and the soldiers fought a little. Meanwhile, soldiers who had received special instructions from the leader cut the ropes on the loads of the ten camels, so that apples spilled onto the ground in all directions.

"And, seeing that it was done, the leader gave the signal and led the retreat.

"The bandits, seeing nothing unusual in their flight, since the bandits themselves were a huge band, began to check their booty. And seeing the apples rolling on the ground, many of them picked them up and ate them.

"So when the troops and merchants returned to the scene, they found the bandits sick and dying everywhere, with only a few capable of fighting. And the leader sent a message to the local amir, instructing him to invade the bandit headquarters and finish off whoever was there.

"And so that is how law and order was accomplished in the place called Dair Gachin."

Zara lay silent for awhile when he had finished. Then she cleared her throat and spoke. "Is that what you're going to do? Poison everyone in the camp?"

Twelve

She was thinking of the old woman who had been so kind to her, and wondered if her own freedom could be worth so many lives.

But then, it wasn't just her life at stake. Like the bandits of Dair Gachin, Jalal had been making trouble for a long time in the Emirates.

"We will not use poison, of course. This camp is full of women and children and other non-combatants. But we can modify the plan. My brothers will try to smuggle in to me some powerful narcotic, and with luck we can put many of them to sleep before we attack. They will also bring in fruit that has been drugged."

She heaved a deep sigh of relief, not realizing how she had communicated her fears to him.

Rafi was silent. "One day, I hope, you will trust me better than this. Do you believe I could allow the unnecessary deaths of so many innocents, Zara?" he asked after a long pause.

"I didn't know." She shifted uncomfortably. "Terrible things do happen, don't they?"

"But this would be massacre. What could justify the massacre of so many of my brother's people? My people, for my brother's people are also my people. Am I such a barbarian in your eyes? What have I done to make you think so?"

She said, "How was I to know? Isn't Jalal a terrible villain? Isn't he a murderer and worse? And aren't all his people implicated with him?"

"No. What has given you this idea? His grandfather was the great bandit Selim. In his day he dominated a part of this desert almost as ferociously as the bandits of Dair Gachin I told you about. But he had no son. He died soon after his grandson came. For twenty five years—most of my life—there was no trouble in the desert.

"Just around the time that we succeeded to our inheritance, his grandson—Jalal—began to cause trouble. He made ridiculous claims for a kingdom carved out of a part of each of the three emirates. He demanded to meet with us to show us the justice of his claims. But his activity at the moment is confined to setting up his camp here, gathering followers to his cause. My brother once laid siege to this fortress, but withdrew without casualties.

"We have known for a long time that he was waiting to get a hostage. Omar discourages tourism in this area, but still, there were opportunities which Jalal did not take. He did not want just any hostage, it seemed. One of us. Not long ago he tried to take my brother Omar's children."

"Are his claims just?"

"Of course they are not. How could they be?"

"What claims did he make? Didn't he even have a pretext?" Zara asked, a little mystified.

"I don't know what his claims may be. We refused to meet with him."

Not believing her ears, Zara struggled out of Rafi's arms and sat up. She stared down at him in the darkness, seeing nothing but the liquid of his eyes in a glimmer of errant moonbeam. "Are you seriously telling me you've got all this trouble with this guy and *you haven't even talked to him?*"

"Zara, my forebears have ruled in this land for hundreds of years. His grandfather was a bandit. What can there be to talk about? If he thinks he has a right to rule because his grandfather was a marauder like the bandits of Dair Gachin, he is mistaken."

"But how do you know what he thinks? You didn't even *talk* to him!" she exclaimed. "You call that diplomacy?"

She could hear by his voice that he was keeping a lid on irritation. "No, I do not call it diplomacy. I do not use diplomacy with bandits. I call this protecting what is my own from those who would steal it. What benefit could there be to me or to my people from negotiations with a bandit?"

"Well, okay, but what's the downside to you and your people from just listening to him?"

"To meet with a man like this is to make the world think he has some right on his side. He has none."

"Why do you care what the world thinks?" she pointed out.

"We trade with the world. If the nations of the West begin to put pressure on me and my brothers to give in to his demands—what could we do?"

"Couldn't you meet with him informally, secretly?"

"We discussed it. We believed that such action on our part would only fuel his determination."

"I thought you said your brother Omar disagreed with that."

"My brother Omar was of the opinion that we should attack quickly and arrest Jalal and his deputies, and disperse his followers. Karim and I did not agree that a pre-emptive strike of this kind was necessary. We see now that we were wrong—and Omar now says that his plan was too extreme, born of bitterness. So you see it is not easy. But Omar was certainly right to this extent—Jalal causes disaffection among the desert tribes. We must deal with him.''

''How?''

He took a deep breath. ''I am not a man who leaps on violence as an alternative, Zara. I and my brothers have the determination to end this situation without violence if possible. We do not want to start by killing. If the answer were merely to kill Jalal and his followers, that would not be difficult to achieve—but violence only opens the door on more violence. Our country now is as blessed as its name. We do not want to go the way of so many others.''

''Oh,'' she said, with a small shamed smile. The smile hid a kind of joy for what she had learned about him.

''The difficulty in this situation is how to free you *without* a killing. If he had harmed you in any way—then I would cut him down without remorse. But within his own lights, he has treated you as well as a prisoner can be treated. Is it so?''

She nodded. When she thought of the vast difference between what her lot as hostage might have been and what it was—Jalal's behaviour could practically be called noble. ''If you're so determined not to start violence, why won't you take it one step further and talk to him?''

''I have told you why not. Talking is not a solution to every problem, Zara. Perhaps you think so, but sometimes it is not the answer.''

''That's just a way of saying I don't understand.''

''Are you so sure that you do understand? It is not a simple issue, and you—''

''And I'm a simple girl?''

''Do not put words in my mouth! I was going to say, you are not very familiar with the history of this problem. How could you be?''

''What you mean is, you don't want to consider a viewpoint not your own.''

''No, that is not what I mean,'' he returned irritably, sitting up himself. He groped in the darkness for a moment, and lit the candle. His eyes flashed in the little glow. "I mean that I have considered this viewpoint—we all did, long ago—and it has too many drawbacks."

"The only thing it has against it is your fear of legitimizing a claim that for all you know may be legitimate to begin with. If the claim is not legitimate, I don't see how listening to it would give it any legitimacy. And if it is legitimate, shouldn't you—"

"I have told you. It is not possible for his claim to have any legitimacy whatsoever."

"Are you telling me there is no conceivable circumstance whereby he might have justice on his side?"

"None whatsoever."

"Then why do you think others will believe it? What are you afraid of?"

"I am not afraid of his claims! I am afraid of his causing diplomatic problems for us that will affect our trade status! Can you understand what a problem it would be for us to refuse to give him sovereignty if the powerful nations threatened our trade? We are not part of OPEC! We are vulnerable to such pressure! I am trying to build roads and houses for my people! There are villages without electricity! My people can be educated in the arts and sciences here, but for technology we still send many abroad! This technological education is critical to our future! Do you ask me to threaten all this by listening to a desert bandit with not enough sense even to…to…to eat green leafy vegetables?"

The ludicrousness of this, delivered as it was in a furious undervoice, struck both of them in the same moment.

"Eat green leafy vegetables?" Zara repeated in a shaky voice, and they suddenly erupted into gusts of laughter and fell into each other's arms and down onto their narrow bed.

The noise of their laughter had to be suppressed, a fact they both instantly remembered. They lay quivering, trying to contain it, while little snickers kept breaking out. Zara pressed her mouth against Rafi's shoulder, and he felt the heat of her breath through the cloth of his shirt and against his skin. Fire erupted in his chest; his body grew hard against her thigh.

"Zara!" he whispered warningly. His hand on her arm tightened, as if to push away from her, or perhaps not.

Zara had also been suppressing more than she knew. Passion seemed to come from nowhere, overwhelming, engulfing her. Suddenly, foolishly, she didn't care about safety, secrecy, life or death. Her blood whispered that the closeness of danger only meant she should take her chance while she had it. That she should snatch at the cup of life while it was so close to her lips...

Of its own accord, her slender hand cupped his dark head. She lifted her upper body on her elbow and smiled down at him, trembling, yearning for him, for his beautiful, flashing dark eyes, for his firm, passionate mouth, for the love and need she saw reflected in both.

"Rafi," she whispered, and bent her head, her hair falling around him like a perfumed cloud, till her sweet, cherry-ripe mouth touched his.

He lifted his hands to stroke her head, he opened his mouth to accept her kiss, both of them drowning in desire. "Sweet," he breathed, "sweet, how I love you."

His mouth was delicious as the fruit they had just shared, sending spirals of delight through her. His hands were strong, thrilling her with his firm possessiveness, his powerful desire. He stroked her cheek, her hair, her back, as his mouth drank in the taste of her.

She was trembling with a feeling that was stronger than anything she had ever felt—a yearning from the deepest part of her self. "Rafi!" she whispered, lifting her mouth. They were in, not a cell, but a magic world bounded only by the edge of candlelight and the black curtain of her hair. There was nothing for her but here, and now.

For him, too. But when he lifted himself, and she turned in his arms to lie beneath him, her chain clanked. It was a loud, unfriendly sound, and she winced as the shackle

chafed her sore skin. It was only a moment's discomfort—
even as she winced she was already holding up her mouth
to be kissed again.

But for Rafi, it was the summons of reason. He closed
his eyes briefly, then opened them again to see her parted,
willing, flame-shadowed lips so close to his; he took a deep,
long, sobering breath, willing his blood to still its storm.

She was smiling at him from passion-darkened eyes. She
was his, he knew it. In this moment it was whatever he
wished. His desire swelled in him for a moment, telling
him that he might never find her so willing again, and he
struggled before he won.

When he knew he had conquered himself, he bent to
plant a light kiss, no more, on those passionately parted
lips. "Zara, this is too dangerous," he said softly. "I dare
not risk it. We must wait."

"Ohhh," she wailed softly, a whisper of complaint. She
lifted a hand to his head, but he caught it and brought it to
his lips.

"You are my treasure. Not this way, Beloved. Not with
you chained to a wall. Shall we give him such a victory?—
that to remember the first time we loved, we must remember this prison and fear and a bandit? That we stole our
pleasure in a moment, not taking time, not making discov-
eries, but snatching at whatever we could reach?"

He was right. She knew, too, that she must not put more
of a burden on him by protesting. She must bring her share
of self-discipline.

She nodded her agreement and struggled to sit up beside
him. "All right," she said.

"We will not regret waiting." His dark eyes promised
much more than he said aloud. "Our patience will be rewarded."

The torment in her blood slowly died. Sanity returned.
The storm passed over them, bringing peace in its wake.
She was hugely grateful to him then. He was more than
right. What would she have thought of him later, if he had

been capable of making love to her for the first time in such conditions?

FROM JALAL IBN AZIZ TO SHEIKH RAFI: I AM IN NO FEAR OF THE SWORD OF ROSTAM OR ANY OTHER. THE SWORD OF JUSTICE IS IN MY OWN HAND. I HAVE STATED MY TERMS. THERE IS NO POSSIBILITY OF COMPROMISE.

Around the camp on three sides and on the far side of the river the military presence was growing, a fact that could easily be seen from the bandit's headquarters. Rows of sand-coloured tents had sprouted like curiously regular dunes. Men moved back and forth. Helicopters came and went and regularly overflew the stronghold in a show of power.

But they were powerless, and all knew it. No mortars could be fired, no bomb dropped, without danger of bringing down the ancient stronghold and killing the hostage.

The bandit's determination to take no hostage but the right one now proved his intelligent foresight. Unless a risk was taken with the hostage's life no conclusion could be forced.

They would take no risk with Rafi's future queen.

There was one press tent. The Barakat Emirates were always news in the West; people liked to keep track of the three handsome princes. Karim and Omar cursed the press presence—one leak, one false report might cost the lives of Zara and Rafi and throw them all into a bloody battle which no one wanted—but they had to put up with it. The press of the world must be seen to be allowed to cover the story.

Omar and Karim had to stand before the press corps on a regular basis, too, briefing them with lies that would protect the mission. Mostly they repeated the same ones over in new words.

The press wasn't happy. They needed some new tidbit

every day to keep the story hot. A waiting game was not a story. They began to ask when and if the princes meant to take action. They could see no reason to wait—unless there was something they hadn't been told. They wanted—although they never admitted it aloud—they wanted the killing to start. Some blood to show the folks back home.

One or two negative stories about the princes were filed. Mostly these were based on the fact that restrictions had been placed on the movements of the press corps, such restrictions being called "anti-democratic." But some began to question the princes' "readiness for battle" and suggested there might be a little question of cowardice influencing their continued waiting. One or two stories suggested that, although each of the princes had served in the military and was commander in chief of his own armed forces, none had ever engaged in an actual campaign.

This last was certainly untrue. At other times Prince Omar's personal sacrifice and bravery during the Parvan-Kaljukistan war on the side of his cousin Prince Kavian Durran had been noted in Western papers—but what was one little misreporting of fact when audience was at stake? So the princes' "failure of nerve" looked like being next up on the agenda. It was only one or two stories so far, but there was nothing the media loved so much as the destruction of heroes they themselves had previously created.

The princes were too involved in their plans to pay much attention to the foreign media coverage, but it did not go unremarked everywhere. Before the trend could gain momentum, a helicopter arrived and, to the delight of the press and the amazement and disapproval of Karim and Omar, disgorged Caroline Langley and Jana Stewart—looking desert chic and lovely, and full of smiles for the mainly male press corps.

Not just smiles. Several cases of chilled champagne were also offloaded from the helicopter, and a couple of palace servants and trays and glasses, and the press corps was invited to toast the engagements and future happiness of these gorgeous Western women who had captured the hearts of princes.

The stories filed that day were all about the beautiful blonde American fiancée of Prince Karim, the beautiful red-headed Scots fiancée of Prince Omar, their plans for a double wedding, which had been delayed by the current crisis, and the champagne on ice they had so thoughtfully brought to the desert campaign....

"What are you doing here?" the princes demanded, when all four were alone together at last.

"Saving you from a public relations disaster," Caroline replied sweetly. "None of those reporters has had alcohol for days! What do you think you're doing?"

Omar almost shouted, "My brother is inside Jalal's camp with his future wife! I have better things to think about than the alcoholic consumption of the press corps!"

"Maybe you do, but somebody had to think about it," Caroline informed her grim-faced future brother-in-law. "We've arranged for supplies to be flown in on a regular basis. Now, we're going to arrange to take the journalists off to do photo shoots of the palaces. And we'll feed them there, and bring them back in a much better mood than they collectively are at the moment."

"They need stories," Jana pointed out firmly before further protests could be lodged. "And you need breathing room. So we're buying you time."

There was one hard-headed, tough and desert-seasoned woman campaigner among the press corps. However much alcohol she might get under her belt, Jana and Caroline were pretty sure that *she* would not be sidetracked by pretty fiancées and palaces.

The woman smelled something. She had already been caught in the no-go area making for the rocky outcrop where the tunnel entrance was hidden. The princes had been very careful not to mark the area as special in any way, and a lot of totally unnecessary Jeep activity went on

in the desert to cover the necessary visits to the tunnel—
but a nose is a nose, and the reporter had one.

If she found the tunnel or even speculated on its existence, a great advantage would be thrown away. Jalal would
certainly close the tunnel, by one means or another, if he
knew they knew of its existence.

On advice from Jana and Caroline, Omar secretly took
this woman aside and promised her an exclusive when it
was over. The price was laying off until they had the hostage safe.

The coming holiday was, they knew, their best chance.
All their efforts were concentrated on that. On the last trip
in with Mustafa, Arif had prevented him taking in all the
fruit the women had asked for. Then Mustafa had promised
faithfully to go in again with the missing supplies on the
very day of the festival.

Men were now engaged in doctoring that fruit with the
drug. There was also a bag of the drug set aside to be given
to Rafi. If they could get this to Rafi during the delivery,
he might be able to put it into the vat of beans that was
part of the traditional fare of the holiday.

That side of the plan was as prepared as possible. The
exploration of the tunnel was more complicated. It might
be as much as two miles long, and there was no way of
knowing how many of Jalal's men might be lurking within.
It would be more than dangerous—it would be foolhardy
to go into it with a light, and virtually impossible to go
without one. The probability of discovery was very high,
and they could not afford to give away their knowledge of
the tunnel by killing a guard.

But unless Rafi discovered for certain that the tunnel ac-
tually debouched into the stronghold, they could not simply
hope to send a squad of men through the tunnel at the
critical moment. What if they emerged into the desert outside the walls?

The tunnel might be a huge advantage, or it might be
worthless. If the drug worked, they could land helicopters

into the compound, but this was an operation that needed ground support.

Rafi had until tomorrow. If he was unable to locate the tunnel entrance in time to inform Arif when he went in with the supply truck, someone would go into the tunnel with an infrared viewer and a tranquillizer gun a few hours before the assault on the place and, with luck, report back. Rafi had timed the shifts of the guards in the compound, and they would make the attempt just as a shift began. That would mean that, with a little luck, anyone they knocked out in the tunnel would not be missed before the assault was made.

But for now it was all waiting.

Thirteen

Early the next afternoon, the old woman entered the prisoner's cell to find her flushed and trembling, her face and hair soaked with sweat, being racked every few moments by dry heaves.

Ah, poor child! What ails thee?

Panting, the prisoner put her hand to her chest. *My heart.*

The old woman dropped to her knees on the floor and laid her ear against the child's chest. Her heartbeat was fast, very fast. She was hot and sweating hard. Gasping for air.

She gently soothed the child's forehead. *Here, drink this water I have brought you.*

The prisoner gratefully drank. Then she mimed a needle going into her arm. *Medicine. I need drugs. Jalal. Tell Jalal.*

If you rest, child, you will feel better soon. And I will bring you…

Drugs! I must have drugs or I will die! Tell Jalal. Bring Jalal. English. English.

The old woman rose to her feet, wailing softly to herself. She set the water within the prisoner's reach, and the little plate of savoury cakes and bits of lamb she had so carefully chosen from the feast food. Then, calling reassuringly that she would bring Jalal, she rushed from the room.

She brushed past the guards and into Jalal's apartments. "Where is he? Where is Jalal?" she demanded of the men lounging there, playing backgammon. They sat up, murmuring in surprise, but before anyone could answer her demand, Jalal himself strode in from the next room.

"What is it?"

"She is dying, the prisoner! Her heart races like a hunted gazelle's. She is asking for you. She says she will die without medicines. She must be released at once!"

"Calm yourself. Young women do not die of heart attacks so easily."

"Go and see her! I insist that you go and listen to what she says! If she dies, you are ruined! We are all ruined!"

Jalal and the old woman stared at each other measuringly. At last he nodded. "Yes, you are right. I will talk to her, find out what the danger is."

He strode out the doors and across the compound. The heat was already intense. Canopies were being erected by a happy group of men and boys all around the perimeter of the open square. They called greetings to him and he nodded and waved as he ducked under the doorway to the passage leading to the prisoner's cell.

"Thank you for coming," she whispered. Her face was covered in sweat, her breathing erratic. Jalal cursed under his breath and knelt by her.

"What has happened?" he asked. He lifted her wrist and felt her pulse. Well over a hundred. Perhaps a hundred and fifty. Jalal sighed. Would fate never support his cause?

"My heart. I—I have a congenital heart defect. Do you know what that is?"

He frowned at her. "Of course I know what—"

Jalal broke off. He blinked rapidly at her, and then gently

bent forward. "I—you—" he murmured. His head sank onto her breast, gently, like a child's seeking comfort.

Zara held her breath as his weight became heavier against her. His hand let go her wrist, and his arm sprawled. His legs unfolded till he was lying flat across her, trapping her arms. "Jalal!" she murmured urgently. "Jalal!"

The bandit did not answer. She shook him again, then struggled to draw her hand out from under him and lifted his eyelid. She saw the white of his eye.

"Unconscious," she said more loudly, raising her eyes as Rafi came up behind. In his hand was a small gun, which he shoved down the waist of his pants. Black, like Jalal's. He bent and lifted the bandit's body off her. It sprawled onto the floor.

"How are you?" he asked anxiously.

Already her breathing was returning to normal. "I'm fine. Don't waste time on me. A half hour of aerobics won't kill me. Can you get his keffiyeh off?"

Perhaps to mark the festive day, Jalal was wearing a green-and-white patterned keffiyeh on his head. With Zara's help, Rafi now pulled it off. He paused, looking into the unconscious face of his enemy.

"My God!" he exclaimed. The resemblance was remarkable.

"Yes, it gives me the shivers," Zara agreed.

In a moment he had wrapped his own head in the borrowed keffiyeh. "Oh, you really are like him!" she exclaimed.

"Good," he said shortly. He pulled the gun from his belt and handed it to her. "Keep that. If he stirs at all, shoot him again. Aim for the chest area, it gives you the biggest target. You have eleven more pellets, but insh'Allah you won't need them all."

"How long—?" she began, taking the gun calmly and weighing it in her hand.

"No one is certain. These things are still experimental

for humans; I am told the results vary greatly. Perhaps two or three hours. Perhaps much less. Be on your guard.''

''What are you going to do?''

''First I will check Jalal's private apartments to see if the tunnel entrance is there. Then I will meet Arif when he comes in with the supplies truck and give him what information I have discovered.'' He pulled a folded piece of paper from his pants pocket to double check it. It was a map showing where he thought the tunnel must be, and where Zara's cell was.

''Do you have your copy of the map?'' he asked.

She nodded, indicating the corner of the mattress where she had placed it.

''I can pass it to Arif without talking to him if necessary, and I will watch where he puts the drug. Then, if all goes well, I will put the drug into the beans. Then I will return here.''

It sounded desperately dangerous, but Zara bit her lip and made no protest. ''And then?''

''You are almost free. A few more minutes and the padlock is broken. Do that while I am away. If the old woman comes, you will have to shoot her, too. You are certain of what to do if I do not return?''

They had plotted and planned late into the night. They had discussed the probabilities and made their best guesses, drawn their maps and made half a dozen contingency plans.

''Yes,'' she said.

He waited, but she said no more. She would not weep or wring her hands or worry anxiously about failure. He bent and saluted her lips with his.

''You are a brave woman,'' he said. A moment later he was gone, leaving her with the unconscious body of his near twin. Setting the gun down close by, Zara picked up the metal file and bent to her task.

''*Salaam aleikum!*'' *Peace be upon thee.*

''*Waleikum salaam,*'' Rafi replied. *And upon thee, peace.*

He raised his hand as he had secretly watched Jalal do, and it occurred to him that the gesture was not unlike his own natural gesture.

He strode across the square towards Jalal's private apartments. Although the perimeter was well guarded, only one place *within* the fortress had a guard—Jalal's own rooms. Two men were on twenty-four-hour guard outside the doors, which lay in the east wing. All that half of the wing was, he thought, otherwise uninhabited.

To a casual observer the two guardsmen might have looked like a formality, like the beaver-hatted guards at Buckingham Palace. But Rafi also had guardsmen in his palace. He knew the difference between those whose duty was a ritual and those whose duty was to guard. These men were always alert. No one ever got near the leader's quarters without being challenged.

Yet he had also seen Jalal himself wandering quite freely in the compound among his people. So his rooms were not guarded because of fears of attempted assassination.

Put all these facts together and there was reason to think that Jalal was keeping the tunnel secret by living over the entrance.

He did not dare to risk his disguise with Jalal's closest companions, who all came and went freely to the private apartments. But there was another area, further along, where men came and went, and Rafi was almost sure that the guards also kept close watch on that entrance. With a casual lifted arm, he strode under the crumbling arches and on towards the heavy wooden door.

Inside, he saw a large, long space supported here and there by pillars. The gloom was relieved by the light of a lantern, beside which sat two men smoking and playing backgammon. They looked up at his entrance. He approached the light quickly so that they would see his face and rely on that for identification rather than his voice. When they saw their leader, they got to their feet in some alarm.

"Shall I saddle Gavrosh, Lord? No one informed us."

A stable! Rafi's heart tightened. That was a reason for the coming and going that he had not thought of. What a miscalculation!

Well, he must risk everything. "Who is on guard in the tunnel?" He spoke raspingly, and coughed as if to clear his throat.

And both men turned as one and glanced into the darkness at the other end of the long pillared room. Rafi closed his eyes with relief. Not wrong after all. The intelligence of the bandit, to disguise his tunnel with his stables!

"Jehan, Ahmad, and Zahir, Lord."

He nodded as if the information meant something, and as his eyes grew accustomed to the gloom he moved slowly down the room towards the total darkness at the end. "What time do they change shift?" His voice was still rough.

He realized he had already begun to enter the tunnel. The floor was sloping down. The darkness was the maw of it. He stood looking blindly in, but it was not the kind of darkness that the eyes grow accustomed to. Too black. He turned around, his eyebrows raised.

His guards shook themselves, recovering from their surprise. "In—at four o'clock, Lord, as usual."

Rafi nodded, and strode towards the door. "Tell Zahir to report to me when he comes up."

"Shall I call him now, Lord?"

His leader turned eyes of surprised disdain on him, and the man bowed jerkily in apology. "I will tell him, Lord, when he comes up."

Rafi went out. In the gloom under the arched overhang, he paused to make notes for his brothers on the back of the map. Then he strolled casually out into the midst of the preparations. He nodded and spoke a word of encouragement here and there, exactly as he would have done for his own people.

He paused by the huge vat sitting over a fire in one

corner, where two or three women stood chatting and stir-
ring. He sniffed the bean stew, and asked for a taste. One
of the women lifted a large wooden spoon from the mixture
and offered it to him, and he bent and tasted it. He smacked
his lips and said it was delicious, and they looked at him,
gratified, but shaking their heads. It was not ready yet! In
another hour, if their Lord cared to eat a portion, they
would not be ashamed then to have their efforts judged,
but now—! They clapped their hands and shook their
heads.

He laughed, swore that it was already clear that it would
be irresistible, promised that he would eat two bowlsful.
"Be sure that you give a bowl to all the guards who have
the misfortune to be on duty today," he commanded. "Let
it not be said that they missed *all* the pleasures of the day."

The women nodded and promised that it would be done.
"We will feed them first!" one promised.

"Excellent," he said, and passed on.

He kept his chin covered by the keffiyeh as far as possible, so that his deficiencies in the area of beard would not
be noted. His moustache was as full as Jalal's.

Before long he was rewarded by the sounds of shouting,
and the main gates were laboriously opened to let in the
battered delivery truck, loaded with crates of fruit. Sitting
beside Mustafa, the driver, wrapped in a heavy keffiyeh, he
was annoyed but not surprised to detect the eyes of his
brother Karim.

It was pure foolhardiness. If Jalal were to trap them both
inside the walls, what choice would Omar have but to ne-
gotiate with the bandit? But Rafi understood the impulse.
He lifted his hands in regal greeting and called a welcome
to the deliverymen. *Noblesse oblige,* and anyway, it was a
holiday.

Karim's eyes widened briefly, and then, taking his cue
from Mustafa, he bowed respectfully to Jalal the bandit. Of
course Mustafa and all his village supported the bandit,
whether from actual political conviction or the simple un-

derstanding that it would be safer for them to pretend to do so.

With a casual eye, Rafi paused to examine the fruit they were offloading, picking up an apple and leaving in its place a piece of paper that instantly disappeared into Karim's hand. "Is this your finest fruit?" he asked.

"The very best we ship," Mustafa assured him, nodding like a puppet. He was terrified that the stranger's presence in his truck would be noticed by the bandit and then both he and his brother would undoubtedly be killed, himself by Jalal and his brother by those who held him hostage. It was a hard life.

Karim said significantly, "Excellent fruit, Lord! Everyone will want to eat it! Delicious, and even better than what was ordered! These grapes, too, are worthy of eating!" He lifted a basket and offered it.

The leader deigned to pluck a grape and taste it. "Excellent! Delicious!" he exclaimed jovially. From across the courtyard the old woman was eying him in amazement.

"What about our guest, my son? Is she well? How did you leave her?" she cried.

My son. Rafi swallowed. Could it be? Women did use the term to young men not related to them…but the tone of voice was not that of an old woman to her leader. He might fool Jalal's people, but if the old woman was truly the bandit's mother—she would not be fooled at close range, nor by the hoarseness of his voice.

In the bottom of the basket of grapes, he knew, was the supply of the drug intended for the stew. The old woman stood gazing at him, waiting for an answer. He glanced at Karim, and saw the knowledge of his danger reflected in his brother's eyes.

Fourteen

The brothers glanced at each other in the full knowledge that it was possible they would both be dead in the next few minutes. Both pairs of eyes glinted with humour and the excitement of danger.

Karim held up the basket of grapes. "Have no fear, Umm Jalal!" he cried. *Mother of Jalal.* It was the way of the desert tribes to call mothers by such an honorific, but if he had supposed wrong... "Even now our leader was asking for the best fruit to take to the sick guest! And I happen to have a beautiful basket of grapes! Your son takes care of all who fall within his shadow, does he not?"

With a large gesture he passed the basket to Jalal, who took them with a nod and turned towards the entrance leading to the passage to Zara's cell. "Now, Mother," he heard Karim's voice behind him. "See what excellencies we have brought for the celebrations today! Are these not fine apples? All the way from the orchards in the hills! Is all in hand for your feast?"

Rafi hurried to the cell. There he found Zara sitting with the kitten in her lap, the gun in her hand, and Jalal's body stretched out neatly on the floor. She jumped up when he appeared in the doorway. "Oh, thank God it's you! Did it all go—"

He interrupted her, putting his fingers to her lips. "We must hurry. We may have only a few minutes and I have to get him hidden."

Zara sobered instantly. "I can help you carry him. I've filed through the padlock."

He put down the basket. "Excellent. Take his feet."

It took them several minutes, and, healthy as she was, she was small, and she was panting when they had finally carried Jalal through to the next room. They quickly returned to her own cell, where Rafi lifted the grapes from the basket, snatched up the plastic bag underneath, and restored the grapes.

"The old woman may come in. If she does, keep her here as long as possible," he said, stuffing the bag of whitish powder into his shirt "The grapes have been brought by Jalal to make you feel better, but he left again immediately. Do you have something with which to tie your shackle on so that she will not notice?"

Zara wordlessly held up a strip of the white dress, carefully dirtied on the floor to make it less visible.

"I will try to let you know when I get back next door. Try and keep her till then if you can. It will be difficult because no doubt she has much to do for the feast. Hide the gun within reach. Don't shoot her with it to keep her here—let her go—but only if there is some other difficulty, such as Jalal awakening. She is Jalal's mother. All right?"

"Good luck," she said with a smile. Underneath she was terrified. The old woman was Jalal's mother? If she saw Rafi at close quarters—or even at a distance! Zara knew she herself could never be mistaken in the identity of the two men now. How much more must that apply to Jalal's own mother! It must not happen.

He disappeared back through the hole in the wall and she was alone. Her heart beating with fear, Zara turned to the business of fixing her shackle on again. The kitten thought it was a game, and did its best to prevent her by biting her fingers and clawing at the ribbon it was used to thinking a toy. But she managed at last.

Then she got up again and did a little quick exercise to boost her pulse rate, keeping a constant eye on the door. The shackle tore at her ankle, and she allowed the tears to come. When she was sweating more than before, she lay down.

So the old woman found her.

How are you now, little one?

"Shokran," Zara said, raising herself on an elbow and smiling through her tears. She didn't want the woman so panicked she would dash off to find her son. *Thank you. A little better.*

The old woman felt her forehead. Still sweaty, but not so much as before, and it was a hot day. She put her head to the prisoner's chest.

Your heart still beats hard.

Zara smiled. She wanted to say, your son is not a big man, but heavy enough, nevertheless. *I am much better. See the grapes that Jalal brought me. Sit and share them with me, please. I am sad.*

Rafi used his pathways through the empty fortress rooms to work his way around to the corner where the bean stew was cooking. There he sat and waited for the moment when the vat would be left unattended. He was wearing his own white keffiyeh now, well wrapped around his head. He did not want to be noticed, and in Jalal's green headgear he would be.

He was relieved to see that the delivery truck had gone. It was a pity he had not spoken to Karim, but all was there in the note. The map, the number of men in the tunnel and above, the timing of the shift. And at the bottom, the words, *Let the first man in bring the Sword of Rostam.*

While he waited, he fitted the bag of soporific inside his shirtsleeve, with the open end rolled up in his cuff at the elbow. All he had to do, he hoped, was pull the plastic free and hold his arm downwards and the drug would pour out.

He could not risk this with anyone watching, but although it was clear that the stew needed little attention now, the women stood around the vat gossiping. He hid in the shadows listening. Over the past few days he had picked up information about the camp in just this way. But now their gossiping made him impatient.

Slowly people began to spill out of the various huts and rooms, dressed in finery. Suddenly one of the women standing over the vat realized that time was passing. "We must go and prepare ourselves for the celebrations!" she cried, and within a minute, all were gone.

The stew was momentarily deserted. Rafi did not wait. He emerged from the shadows and slipped under the canopy that sheltered the vat from the sun. Its rays were reduced in intensity now; it was lower in the sky. This corner of the yard was already full of shadows.

He leaned over the vat for a moment, a man curious about the traditional dish, stirred it as if absently, and then was gone.

Zara was trying, with her dress fabric, to fashion a little sling in which to take out Mr. Wriggly when the time came. Going into the next room to check on Jalal, she had noticed the remnants of her dress and carried it back with her. She tore the top of the dress off, and tied the two sleeves together to form a long strap. She was hoping that she could somehow tie the kitten snugly into the bodice—and as long as she left his head out, perhaps he wouldn't struggle too wildly. And by slinging it over her shoulder or neck, she would leave her hands free.

But exactly when to try to tie him into it would be the

problem. If she did it too soon, he would go crazy all tied up. If she left it too late…there would be no time if he struggled.

It was so difficult to tell how long Jalal would sleep. He had not stirred, but she shot him with the tranquillizer gun again anyway. The timing of the enterprise was all dependent. Rafi had to wait until people started to show the effects of eating the drug, then signal his brothers.

They were going to attack tonight whether the drug worked or not. There would never be a better time. But if the drug had not worked they were expecting bloodshed.

The worst of it was that the plan kept being modified in the light of events. Rafi had to be constantly thinking on his feet. Having found the tunnel entrance, he had told her he thought that during the party there might be a way to take Zara out by way of the tunnel before the attack started. For that, though, she would need a disguise. He could take her through a deserted part of the fortress some of the way, but still there would be twenty yards or more to cover in the open.

He was looking for a possible disguise now, while also waiting for the bean dish to be served and eaten. But all the women were wearing their beaded headscarves and embroidered tunics at the party. Zara would be noticed if she went out in someone's ordinary clothes. Most of the women had only one or two sets of clothes, and were recognized at a distance by what they wore. He was cursing himself for not having foreseen the need for a disguise.

The sun was low in the sky, Zara could tell. Should she tie the kitten into the bag now? Surely one way or the other, Rafi would be coming for her very soon? If only she had asked for a little of the drug to give to the kitten!

She heard a noise behind her and turned to greet him. What she saw instead was the barrel of an automatic pointing straight at her eye. "Get up," said Jalal softly. "Make no noise. I will not hesitate to kill you."

* * *

They were dropping like flies, Rafi saw with satisfaction. Lying under the canopies, one after the other they set down the bowl of beans, yawned and stretched out for a nap. The guards, too.

He was watching from the roof. When he was satisfied that the effects would be widespread, he turned and gave the signal. It was quick, but repeated until he got the answering code. It came quickly.

Now he had to get down to Zara's cell, on the opposite side of the central square. He took the fastest way, around the roof to a staircase. From there it was a dangerous climb down a broken-down, almost impassable stairwell.

He saw them emerge below him, Zara with her hands tied behind her, Jalal forcing her to run, holding her up, when she stumbled, cruelly, with the bonds that held her wrists. They were zigzagging under and between the arches heading towards the tunnel.

Standing on the roof, Rafi pulled his gun from its holster and fired into the air. "Jalal!" he screamed.

Behind a pillar, the bandit turned his head, saw his enemy high above. He pulled Zara around to put her between them, and began dragging her backwards. He saluted Rafi, the gun barrel just touching his forehead. "Another time!" he cried. "I have pressing business."

He had no clear shot and he knew he wouldn't get one. Cursing, Rafi shoved the gun back on his hip and began the wild precipitous descent down the half-destroyed stairwell. By the time he had reached the ground there was no sign of them. He ran across the courtyard towards the tunnel. All around him men and women lay snoring. Some tried to get up, staggered and fell.

His brothers must have sent the troops down the tunnel long ago. They would have been in position, waiting for the signal. Jalal would never get out with her, it was impossible.

Yet still he ran.

He heard the sound of hoofbeats, and the next moment

a large black horse charged straight for him, knocking him
down, sending his gun flying. On its back was Jalal, with
Zara slung over the horse in front of him, face down. It
was an exact replay of the first time he and Jalal had met.
He vowed the bandit would pay for it.

Rafi dived for his gun, and chased the horse on foot, but
the bandit knew his stronghold better than Rafi could. By
the time Rafi had him in his sights, Jalal had opened a small
door inset into the main gate and was bending low over the
horse to go through. With a curse, Rafi aimed at the horse.

His gun jammed, damaged somehow by its fall. In a few
seconds Jalal was galloping off over the desert, now glowing pink in the setting sun.

Rafi ran back towards the stable and the tunnel entrance.
Surely there was more than one horse in the bandit's stable!
Even on the thought, he heard the sound of horses. He
entered the stable again to see, emerging from the tunnel
at a near gallop, his Companions, in twos and threes,
mounted on their horses.

First was Arif, leading Rafi's own black, Raksh.

"Lord!" he cried, dismounting as the others pulled up.
"We heard the shot and knew that stealth was unnecessary.
What's toward?"

"They are asleep, all save Jalal himself. He has taken
Zara and galloped into the desert," Rafi shouted, as he
mounted into the saddle. "Who follows?"

"A platoon of foot, on the run. The way has been
lighted, the guards subdued. We will go with you, Lord, to
bring her back!" the Companions cried.

On Rafi's saddle hung the Sword of Rostam, not in its
ceremonial, but in its battle scabbard. Rafi pulled the strap
over his head, settled the sword on his hip, and urged his
mount into a gallop.

The Companions followed him, out into the square,
around, and then through the gate and out into the desert.
Ahead of them, his horse's fine black tail streaming in the

wind as he urged it across the broken desert, Rafi drew the gleaming scimitar from its scabbard.

"Ya Rostam!" he cried.

It was the traditional battle cry of his forebears when they drew the Sword of Rostam against an enemy.

"Ya Rostam!" they answered. Then, as one man, the Companions of Sayed Hajji Rafi Jehangir ibn Daud ibn Hassan al Quraishi lifted their heads and opened their throats in the high yodelling cry of their warrior ancestors.

They galloped at full tilt, following their prince, crying their bloodchilling battle cry to the vengeful winds. Now it was a battle to the death.

Fifteen

Trucks and Jeeps were rolling ponderously across the desert from the highway to the south to surround the fortress. Jalal spurred his mount towards the cluster of villages a few miles to the north. The people there supported him, would receive him and hide the hostage.

He glanced back over his shoulder. A troop of horse burst from the gates and spread out across the red desert. He cursed the sun for not setting faster. A few more minutes and he would have been lost in the shadows. As it was, he cast a huge shadow. They were already coming after him.

His horse was hampered by the double burden. He would never make the villages. Jalal changed direction and made towards the biggest rocky outcrop within reach.

Zara was spending most of her energy on trying to keep conscious. Folded over the horse as she was, its sweating odour choking her, her stomach being jolted unmercifully, in terror of slipping off under the deadly hooves, she was so sick with nausea and fear that she could feel the constant drag of a faint. She was sure that would be fatal. Jalal was gripping her with one rough hand on her bound wrists, but still it needed all the effort of her stomach muscles to cling on.

She could not see where they were going, her view restricted to the tirelessly galloping hooves and desert floor. When she lifted her head her hair fell in her eyes, she could see nothing. Her last sight of Rafi had been as he was sent sprawling almost underfoot by Jalal's kick. She had seen his gun go flying, but nothing more, and he was frozen there in her mind's eye, in the act of falling, the gun on the air, dust everywhere, like some horrible photograph of war.

The sound of the horse's hooves was too close to her ears, but she thought she heard helicopters behind them, and the strangely melodious howling of animals, like the coyotes at night when she went camping in Algonquin Park. She had always loved that plaintive, lonely sound, and it comforted her now, without reason.

The horse stopped with a jerk that was so unexpected and so final she fell. But Jalal had already dismounted in time to catch her, and before she knew it she was running wildly up a rocky incline, forced to leap a chasm that terrified her, dragged further. Her bare feet were cut and bleeding, she saw, but she strangely felt no pain. Her arms, too, were mercifully numb. Her clothes were torn in several places, and stained with dirt and blood, but she had no idea where the blood came from. She didn't care. If she was going to get out of this alive, she had to keep her mind clear and watch for opportunity.

He dragged and pushed her up and up. Her ascent was difficult at all times, because her bound arms meant she had poor balance, but it was worst when he dragged her backwards, clasping her arm or sometimes her bound wrists.

Suddenly, below on the desert floor, she saw the horse-

men and learned that that wild comforting cry came from
their throats. One of them gazed upwards for a moment, a
curving sword held high in his hand. It glowed blood red
in the setting sun, and she shivered in primitive horror before she understood.

"*Rafi!*" she screamed.

She watched as he methodically sheathed the sword and
then dismounted from his snorting, stamping horse. Then
he ran towards the thrust of rock that the desert had some-
time, long ago, spewed up. Jalal's gun exploded near her
ear and the bullet pinged off the rocky slope below, but
Rafi had already disappeared from view.

Jalal dragged her more quickly then. She thought he was
heading for some known place, and wondered what it was.

"You can't possibly win this," she said breathlessly.
"Why don't you give up now? If you do, Rafi will talk to
you about your claim, I'm sure he will."

"I am sure he will, too," came his dry voice. "When
he realizes that you are my hostage and will be so until we
meet—he and his brothers and I."

On the desert floor, Rafi briefly directed his Companions
to try to scale the rocks at a variety of places around the
perimeter, then turned to make the ascent himself. Arif
stopped him. "You have no gun, Lord! Take mine!" he
said, thrusting his own revolver into Rafi's holster. "The
bullets in your holster are the wrong calibre," he said then.
"Take my holster, too."

Rafi impatiently shook his head. "No time for that. How
many bullets in the gun?"

It was an automatic. "Nine," said Arif.

Rafi nodded. "I hope to need only one."

"Lord—" But the prince had already begun the climb.
Arif waited till he had mounted a few yards and then followed.

Zara understood Jalal's choice as soon as they arrived at
the place. They were within a couple of yards of the sum-

mit, a large plateau that seemed to fall away steeply on all sides except that of their approach.

At the last he led her up a steep incline and edged through a narrow passage between two high sheets of rock that admitted only one. Immediately they were faced with another chasm, three feet wide, not very deep, but sharply precipitous. Anyone falling down it would break ankles at least. For someone hurled down with their arms bound, death was more likely.

He made her leap it. She screamed in terror as she went, but somehow they both made it to the other side. There, they landed on a small shelf. It was perhaps a couple of yards square in the centre, quickly tapering to the merest toe hold at each end. There was a man-sized niche in the rock leading up to the plateau, and now Jalal stood inside it. He was protected on three sides. In front of him, he held Zara, facing the passage which was the only angle of approach. At her feet, a few feet away, was the chasm. One push would send her staggering helplessly over the edge.

She was panting with exertion and terror. If Rafi came through that little defile, he was an unmissable target. And if he was following them, he would come through. "Rafi!" she screamed, "no closer!"

She cringed, expecting a blow from the gun on her head, but he merely growled, "Shut up! He must come and he knows it."

"Don't kill him," she pleaded. "Please don't kill him."

Jalal looked down and their eyes met. "Don't kill *him?*"

"Please, please."

"He chooses his bride well, at any rate," Jalal said.

"I am his bride," she said urgently. "I am going to marry him. Let me go, and I will convince him to talk to you. He will give you a hearing if I ask him to do it."

He laughed. "You are a woman who should be believed when she says she can make a man do a thing," he observed mildly. "But I prefer my own way. I petitioned and was not heard. Now I beg for the princes' favour no longer. Now I dictate.''

"Please let me go. If you don't, you know there will be blood shed. Someone will get hurt. He told me that they are determined not to shed blood. But if you do this— please, it's so dangerous.''

"My people lie dead, and you say they were determined to hurt no one?'' Jalal laughed. "Their determination did not last long!''

"But they're not dead, they're asleep!'' she cried. "It's a drug!''

He stared at her, frowning.

"Why do you think *you're* alive? He could have killed you more easily—instead he shot you with a tranquillizer gun! If he had killed you we wouldn't be here now. I'd be safe, and you'd be dead.''

"My people are not dead?''

"I swear it. I swear it on my life.''

There was tense silence for a time she could not count. Then they heard the scraping of boot on rock. "Rafi, no!'' she screamed again. "Go back!''

Jalal snorted, and called out, "Your woman imagines you to be a coward, Rafi, Prince of the Realm! Are you so?''

Zara gasped as Rafi stepped negligently into perfect target range between the two upright shafts of rock. "I am here, Jalal grandson of Selim the Bandit,'' he said. "What now?''

The light was fading; blood red shadows were everywhere. Zara felt the metal of the gun brush her forehead, and Jalal's grasp on her bound hands tightened.

"Throw your gun down,'' Jalal ordered.

As if it meant nothing, Rafi lifted the gun from his holster and tossed it into the rocky ravine at his feet.

"And what now, Jalal the Bandit? *Bien aimée, tu m'entends,*'' Rafi spoke the first phrases clearly, drawled them almost, then added the next sentence in a quick mutter she almost didn't catch.

Beloved, you hear me. He was speaking to her in French.

"How many of my people are dead, Rafi son of Daud?" Jalal asked.

"We killed none, Jalal son of Aziz. Three in the tunnel were wounded, but not mortally. All that you saw on the ground were drugged. They will recover without ill effects."

Zara felt him relax and knew that he had accepted it. She heaved a sigh of relief.

"Let her go, and we will talk," Rafi said.

"I will not let her go, but I will not kill her, either. I want a helicopter immediately, to land on the rock above my head. One pilot only inside."

Rafi laughed. "A helicopter! Where will you go? There will be no escape, Jalal. *Watch his gun hand.*"

Again the quick phrase added in French. She looked from one to the other. In the deepening gloom, their physical resemblance was even more remarkable.

"There is no escape for you either, Prince of the Realm! We will deal together sooner or later, you and your brothers and I!"

"We will never deal together unless you give her to me now. Take her from here and you lose everything," Rafi said firmly.

"I will give her up after we have negotiated. Do you think I will pass her to you on the basis of your word? What good is your word to me? You and your brothers have violated all other bonds, why should your word be good?"

"You may trust me in this. We will talk with you, but you must first give her up. *When his aim wavers I will jump.* Let her come to me now, and we will all go back to the palace and we can discuss whatever you wish. *Prepare.* If not, what can your destiny be but a prison cell?"

''If you speak to the hostage in French again I will throw her over the edge,'' Jalal said coldly.

Rafi's eyebrows went up in surprise. ''Ah, we heard that you were an educated man. Did you go abroad to study?''

''You know well the answer to that.''

I know? Rafi frowned, at a loss for a moment.

''It grows darker. You have not summoned the helicopter. Do you have a mobile phone, a walkie-talkie?''

Rafi lifted his hands. ''Neither. What can I do? Perhaps we should wait till morning.''

She felt Jalal's amused laugh. ''Your loyal Companions are all around you, no doubt. Summon the nearest and pass on the message. If there is no helicopter waiting above me before the sun sets, I will shoot this beauty and throw her over the edge. It would be a loss. She pleaded for your life, not her own. How many women will you find of such character? You choose, Prince of the Realm.''

''And what then? Do you think we would ever talk to a murderer about his claims to a heritage?''

''Summon me the helicopter before the sun sets or watch her die. Or perhaps, see her live a cripple. You have perhaps three minutes, perhaps four.''

He was steely. Zara could feel the determination in him, and was afraid.

Rafi raised his voice. ''Arif!''

''Lord!'' came the faint cry behind him.

''You are in contact with my brothers?''

''I am, Lord.''

''Tell them to send a helicopter. To the top of the rock above our heads. The pilot only inside.''

There was a pause, a murmur. Then, ''It is done, Lord.''

In the distance the sound of an engine changed. One of the helicopters hovering over the fortress had changed course. In the shadows, Rafi dislodged a piece of the loose rock under his hand.

''Well, then, bandit. Your helicopter comes. What next?''

"You know already, Prince. She goes with me. If you wish to see her again, you know the way."

The helicopter must have been closer than they knew, flying low to the ground, the sound diminished by the wall of rock. Suddenly, with a loud roar, it roared up and appeared almost directly overhead. Jalal glanced up, no more, but for the first time the gun was not pressed against her temple. Quick as lightning, Zara opened her mouth and with all her strength bit into his wrist.

He cried out in surprise and looked at her. In the next moment, Rafi leapt onto the ledge and smashed the rock down on Jalal's fingers. The gun went flying down into the ravine. Feeling herself released, Zara dropped to her knees before he could take another hold on her, and crawled sideways out from between the two men. She saw the last blood red glitter of the sun on the blade of the Sword of Rostam as its deadly beauty whipped from its sheath.

"I warned you it would be a fight to the death, Jalal grandson of Selim," Rafi said, placing the sword against his enemy's neck, flattening him against rock.

"Don't kill him, Rafi!" she whispered helplessly.

Jalal stood straight and looked him in the eye. He smiled. "So be it, then, Rafi son of Daud. But beware your father's curse if you kill your brother's son."

Sixteen

Zara stretched and yawned luxuriously as the door opened softly and a woman in a white polo shirt and green pants entered. She crossed to the table, paused and leaned over Zara. "Oh, good, you're awake. Did you have a lovely massage?"

"Lovely," Zara agreed.

"Ready for your facial?"

"Mmmm."

The woman, a beautician named Maria, moved some wheeled trays around and then seated herself at Zara's head.

"Same as yesterday, or something new again?"

Zara smiled. "Something new again."

"How about a cucumber mask?"

"Sounds divine."

"I met Sheikh Rafi a few minutes ago. He just arrived. He asked how you're feeling today, and I told him barring a few abrasions you're pretty much back to your old self. He's expecting you for dinner, did you know?''

"Yes, I got the summons earlier." Zara smiled.

"He's incredibly dishy, isn't he?''

Dishy, she knew, was the English for *gorgeous.* "Incredibly.''

"Don't you feel lucky?''

Zara laughed delightedly. "Yes, I feel amazingly, fabulously lucky that such a wonderful man wants to marry me, of course I do! I've seen him in better and in worse, and there is no one in the world like him. In the universe, probably. And on top of everything else, he lives in a palace! I keep hoping I won't wake up!''

"Well, don't talk anymore, and I'll do my best to make sure you're as beautiful as can be tonight. It won't be hard. Adilah is doing her bit, too. She has some of the loveliest costumes I've ever seen in my life for you to try on. She was showing them to me. They really know how to live out here, don't they?''

It had all been just as Rafi had promised, right down to the portrayals of Shirin and Khosrow on the walls of the bath. She had been pummelled, pampered and cosseted, her wounds had been doctored, her hair expertly trimmed, her nails manicured. She had swum and lazed in the sun. She had been fed the most delicious foods. She had gone for walks in the mountains. She had even been taken through her paces by a fitness trainer.

She had discovered the lifestyle of the idle rich, and pretty fabulous it was.

It had lasted four days so far, during which she recuperated in the palace, while Rafi and his brothers had talks with Jalal in the capital, Barakat al Barakat. Except for the staff, she had been alone. Then Caroline Langley and Jana Stewart, introducing themselves as "the other two fiancées," had flown in to visit her. They had stayed one night and most of a day and had departed again only this morning.

This morning…after Rafi sent word that he would be home and hoped to see her over dinner. Zara had heard from excited staff that he had sent orders to the kitchen for a magnificent meal for two.

Zara was nervous, excited, terrified, happy. She had never looked forward to a man's arrival with such nervous delight, such hungry anticipation, such longing, such… bridal jitters. When she thought of him, she seemed to step into a river of flowing sensuality, of rich loving need, that poured over and through her, leaving her helpless.

She loved him. It was hard for her now to remember that time—only days ago!—when she had worried that the feelings she had for him might be a result of her solitary confinement and unstable emotions. She had no doubts now. When she had stood at the precipice and thought that Jalal might kill him…everything had been clear as a running brook. She had known then that her life could never be other than bleak if Rafi died. That something so wonderful and precious as her future with Rafi must not be allowed to disappear before she had even had a chance to know it.

He had not died. Instead he had discovered a relative he didn't know he had—and now, after sorting out Jalal's future, he was coming home. To her.

"Stop smiling, you'll crack your mask," Maria implored her. "It's just drying nicely." Rafi had flown in an entire team from a top English spa hotel for two weeks, no doubt at huge cost, and they were all enjoying their stay in the palace enormously. Zara had given them the freedom of the swimming pool and tennis courts, and often they joined her there along with the archaeological team, who had also come to spend a day and a night having facials and massages. They had all quickly become friendly.

They were all envious, of course—who could help envying such fabulous luck? But no one wished her anything but good. She was friendly and easy, and everybody could see why Rafi had chosen her—she had something special, the spa team agreed with Zara's old friends. Something more than just the petite, perfect build, the wonderful hair, the gorgeous, warm eyes, the mesmerizing smile... Zara was the kind of enchanting woman who *should* be a princess.

"Everybody's saying there's going to be a triple wedding ceremony, all three of the princes at once. Is that true?" Maria asked, forgetting that she had forbidden Zara to speak.

The three fiancées had discussed it, but a lot depended on things like security; they were all aware it might not be viable. But it would be an occasion if they could do it, all right! Zara parted her lips the merest quarter of an inch and then spoke without moving a muscle. "Not sure," she said. "Hear ut Ravi says tonight."

"Well, I think it would be absolutely fabulous if you did! I gave them both facials yesterday, and they're terrific, aren't they? Did you know them from before?"

She carefully laid a warm cloth over the mask, and Zara could feel it instantly softening. "No, it was the first time."

Half an hour later she got up from the table feeling relaxed and just a little like a finely tuned, well-oiled machine, and rinsed off with a shower. Then she went to her "apartments," where her personal maid, Adilah, awaited her. Adilah was still thrilled with her sudden promotion up the palace ranks, and was learning English as fast as she could.

On the bed and couches of Zara's half-acre bedroom she had spread out several exotic, beautiful outfits for Zara to choose from, each outfit coordinated with its own pair of sandals, shoes or slippers. Zara felt she had done nothing but smile for four days, and as she stood and looked around her own private Aladdin's Cave, the smile pulled her mouth again.

Lustrous silks, spangled gauzes, jewelled belts...a bright rainbow of colours so glowing it was as if a candle secretly flamed behind everything. In fact, that was how her life felt—as if a candle had been set inside a simple glass vase, and suddenly it was revealed as intricately cut and decorated, glowing and glittering like a precious jewel.

With Adilah's help, she chose a lustrous *shalwar kamees* in a delicate transparent silk of midnight blue underlaid with glowingly soft grey silk satin and spangled with tiny silver stones, with a low scoop neckline and flowing skirted tunic over trousers of the same fabric. A long spangled gauzy midnight-sky scarf for her neck, and delicate mules with a one-inch heel, in the softest leather she had ever touched, also in deep blue, for her feet.

"Lovely, lovely!" murmured Adilah, as she stood back to admire her handiwork. She had been practising her English with the spa team. "Absolutely smashing, Madame."

Zara examined herself in the mirror. Her hair was shining and healthy, spreading in its curling mass over her shoulders and down her back to her waist. Her face glowed with expensive, subtle cosmetics, her eyes sparkling, her mouth a warm peach.

She had no earrings or jewellery of her own, of course. She had come here like the beggarmaid, with nothing. Whatever jewellery she had been wearing on the night of the kidnapping had been long since lost. She could not remember what it had been, anyway. The emerald wishing ring was on her right hand, and as for the left—well, if Rafi wanted to do something about that, she would need nothing more. She thought he would do that tonight.

Dinner was to be served in the dining room of her own apartments, and she went there a few minutes before time to check the arrangements. It was enchanting. She examined the table and the flowers, but all was perfection, and she moved out to the fountained court. She was somewhere in the centre of the palace, she knew, but in the courtyard you were aware of nothing but mountains. The sun was setting off to the south, the full moon already visible in the sky above the high peaks to the north and east, the air clear, cool and fresh and smelling of perfume, and just a little, unless it was her imagination, of the snow still capping the peaks high above her.

The fountain in the centre spilled water in an endless rippling music. All around the perimeter, bordering the roofed walkway like a medieval cloister, were perfect arches, decorated in painted blue mosaic tiles. At every arch there was some flowering plant.

Her enchanted castle. She heard a sound and turned, and the prince entered the Enchanted Castle.

He too was dressed in the Eastern style, a green silk tunic embroidered from the cuffs to the elbows and on the high collar with magnificent gold thread and jewels, loose flowing trousers. He had shaved off his new beard, but his flowing moustache still curled over his upper lip. He reminded her of the night of his feast in the desert, that seemed so long ago.

She stood beside the fountain gazing at him with love and longing, a smile pulling irresistibly at the corners of her mouth.

Rafi did not smile. He stood for a moment looking at her, too moved to smile. She was his, he knew it without her having to speak the words. She would not be here, she would not be smiling, she would not be dressed in this way, if her answer were no. He had spent the last four days torn between wishing and fearing to come to her, finding it nearly impossible to concentrate on the negotiations, until his brothers had sent him away. Even Jalal had agreed that it was useless to talk until Rafi had had his answer from his Beloved.

Birds were singing evensong. The moon was growing brighter as the sun died in the west. The sky darkened and stars came out to match those that spangled in her eyes and on her dress. His heart leapt from him and went to her, and he knew he would never have it back again.

He followed his heart across the space between them, and stood gazing into her steady eyes. He knew everything about her, and yet not enough. He would spend his life in the discovery of her magic, her beauty, her generosity, her nobility.

His hand touched hers, and they trembled. He lifted it and drew it onto his other palm, lowered his head to kiss it. His thick dark hair fell forward, and she saw it trembling with the power of his feeling. She knew she had never met a man of such honour, such truth, such bravery, such generosity of spirit. She had never loved before with all of her being. Helpless to express her knowing, she bent her own head and kissed his.

He felt the kiss on his hair as if it connected him to the deepest river of being, and then they raised their heads and their lips met at last, and the river ran through them, a rich, wild torrent.

"Beloved," he said.

"I love you, Rafi," she said, marvelling at the layers of meaning those words now had, beyond all ordinary understanding, knowing he understood.

"I will love you all my days. I will take no wife but you," he said.

He did not ask her, because he knew. And for her, too, that was as it should be. How could there be doubts or questions between them, when they knew everything with a touch?

"I will take no husband but you," she said.

They walked in the garden, while the moon climbed the sky and the stars burned brighter and the sky darkened to black. The birds finished their song, and a flower wantonly released her perfume as if the night air itself were her lover. They spoke and were silent, touched and did not touch, and it was all the same because they were enclosed in love.

Inside, behind the glass, soft lamps were lighted, and figures moved around the table, preparing for their meal. At last they went in.

The two servants turned and bowed.

Rafi took Zara's hand in his. "Hanifah, Hayat," he said,

calling each by name, and they bowed again. "I know you for true believers," the prince said.

The women bowed again. "It is so, Lord."

"Bear witness that I take your mistress as my wife," he said, and then he turned and smiled at Zara and repeated the words in English.

The women stood shy and speechless, smiling but over-awed by their magnificent master and their beautiful mistress, now their queen.

Rafi spoke again. "We are husband and wife now," he said. "Whatever ceremony we choose to have later for the sake of my people and yours—between you and me and God, we are married here and now. This is the tradition and the law. We are one already. We declare it before two persons. Do you accept this?"

Tears burned her eyes. "Yes, I accept it," she said.

He turned again to Hanifah and Hayat and spoke a few words, and they bowed and left the room. Rafi led her to a low couch and seated her on it, and only then did she see the flat boxes on the little carved table nearby.

"I asked Adilah what you had chosen to wear tonight," he said by way of explanation, opening the first box. It was large, thick and square, and inside, on creamy satin, lay a magnificent collar of pearls and sapphires, like nothing she had seen before.

"Ohhh, Rafi!" she breathed helplessly.

He picked it up and slipped it around her neck. Five equal rows of pearls snugly encircled her neck, with one massive sapphire in the centre, and beneath, three more giant sapphires, linked by delicately worked platinum en-twining smaller sapphires and pearls, fanned out over her upper chest. The other boxes revealed matching drop ear-rings and a staggering bangle bracelet studded with sap-phires all around its circumference.

Zara stood and went to a mirrored pillar to admire.

"I've never worn anything so beautiful," she breathed.

"They have never been worn by anyone so beautiful,"

he returned. "They have been the property of the women of my family for many generations, but I think the jeweller was thinking of you as he crafted them."

They made her brown eyes appear black. Nothing had ever done that before. Zara closed her eyes and shook her head a little. She turned her back on the mirrored pillar and faced him. "This isn't a dream, is it?"

He rose and crossed to her. "Does it feel unreal to you, Beloved? It feels very, very real to me."

She smiled and shook her head. "Not unreal. But as though...as though I've been taken on a magic carpet to a place where—" she struggled to explain "—where my life never expected to be. And now that it's there, everything has changed."

He was smiling at her. "Yes, like Prince Tanbal and the magic horse. I will tell you the story one day. Then you will see that the best life is one that offers you a ride on a magic carpet to unknown places—if you accept the ride."

She moved closer to him and he put his arms around her. "Will you tell me that story tonight?"

"Tonight? No. Tonight I will tell you other things, Beloved."

"What things?"

"The love that I have longed to tell you since that day when I saw you in the waterfall," he said simply. She closed her eyes as feeling swamped her. Her heart seemed to be pouring with light, love, joy too wonderful to speak.

"I love you," she moaned helplessly.

"I love you. I want you now to choose a ring, as is traditional for Westerners. Come."

He led her back to the sofa and when they were seated again, he opened the last box, a huge flat box with the name Van Cleef & Arpels embossed in the velvet. Inside were about twenty-five magnificent rings.

She swallowed in amazement. "You just have a whole boxful of engagement rings?" she whispered.

Rafi laughed lightly. "The jeweller has sent these for you

to make your choice. In the future you will learn many of the rituals of me and my people, but I follow this Western ritual as testament that I and perhaps my people, too, will also learn some of your own customs. I know in your country a woman likes to receive an engagement ring. If these are not enough to choose from, they will quickly send more.''

Well, she had seen things like this in elegant windows, of course, but she had not ever dreamed of having such a tray placed before her with the instruction to choose among them. Choose a ring to treasure for all the rest of her life as a symbol of the moment when she knew she loved and was loved.

The wonderful stones danced and melted before her eyes. They were arranged in rows—the diamonds, the rubies, the sapphires, the emeralds—all so cunningly crafted, so enticingly beautiful, how could she choose…? There was a huge heart-shaped ruby embedded amongst close-set diamonds in a wide curving band, and she smiled, catching sight of it.

''Oh, how—it's breathtaking!'' she whispered, her fingers just touching it.

His darker, fine-boned hand came down and firmly lifted the ring from its velvety bed. ''This one?'' he murmured, as if the choice appealed to him, too.

He lifted her hand in his and slipped the ring over her knuckle and down to a firm home at the base. Of course during all the various massages and treatments someone had sized her finger, she realized with a smile.

''It's beautiful,'' she said again, wondering again at the levels of meaning an ordinary word could have, all unknown to those who had not experienced its true depths. ''A heart-shaped ruby, though! People will say it's…''

''People will say we're in love,'' he said. And he kissed her, and the choice was made.

At last they made their way to the table, and the feast was brought in.

When they had talked of all and everything for awhile, and taken some of each luscious dish the chef had cooked to perfection, she remembered his mission of the past few days, and her confinement, and the bandit.

"Tell me about Jalal," she said then. "Who is he? What happened? What did you decide?"

"You know that Jalal is the grandson of Selim. His mother—the woman who looked after you during your imprisonment—is Selim's daughter." Rafi took a breath, and spoke more slowly. "His father, however, was my brother Aziz, who was killed the year before we were born." Zara's lips parted in astonishment, and forgetting his story, he broke off to draw her hand to his lips.

"Please go on, this is as good as King Mahmoud any day!"

"Aziz fell in love with the bandit's daughter and was afraid to tell my father. But when she told him she was pregnant he promised to tell my father and seek permission to marry her. He was killed two days later."

"Oh, how—!" She thought again of that moment when she was afraid Jalal would kill Rafi, her anguish at the thought of losing him before they began. She broke off, closed her eyes and shook her head.

"Then what?"

"It is difficult to be sure what happened next. Jalal's mother told her father. She was lucky not to be killed outright for shaming the family, but old Selim was not a bandit for nothing. He understood the supreme importance of the baby his daughter was carrying. He married her to an old man to protect her name and so she was able to give birth and remain with the tribe. And her father made his plans. But whatever they were, they were disrupted first by the birth of my father's three new sons, and then by the bandit's own death. Her old husband also died. So she was left alone with her child."

"And then?"

"And then one day, this woman—her name is Nusaybah—got her courage up, made her way to the palace, and insisted on talking to someone. She says she talked to an old man close to the king—it sounds like Nizam al Mulk, my father's Grand Vizier, but at this distance in time, it's impossible to be sure. She was sworn to secrecy, which included an embargo on telling her son the truth.

"She and her child were given a place to live with their wants supplied, and she says that from that time Jalal's education was supervised and paid for. She herself was also taught to read. But she never met the old man again. Documents would come informing her of what was planned for her son, and off he would go to school or college or the armed forces."

"My God, is it possible?"

"We believe it. They are testing our DNA at the moment, but we do not doubt what he and his mother tell us. There is too much evidence."

"But then—why didn't he just tell you? Why all the mystery?"

"He believed we knew."

"He believed you *knew?*"

"Two or three times my brother Omar had the chance to kill him. He did not do so. Once in the desert he even laid siege to the fortress for three weeks without a shot being fired. Jalal saw this as evidence that Omar was unwilling to risk my father's curse."

"And that wasn't the reason?"

"No. Or not as far as Omar knows. Who knows what may be hidden in the deep layers of the mind? But Omar was not long back from the war in Parvan then. Although he started out with ruthless determination, he said when he got to the fortress siege he could not stand to take part in any more bloodshed and eventually lifted the siege. Jalal of course was meanwhile bringing in supplies through the tunnel.

"Omar has no explanation for why he did not pull the trigger on two other occasions when he had Jalal in his sights. Perhaps because Jalal resembles me. Perhaps not.'' He shrugged. ''Is there a deeper meaning behind such things?''

Zara's eyebrows moved together in thought. ''Did your father's curse include Jalal, then?''

''We did not understand it so at the time, of course. But his words were—if any of my sons takes up arms against any brother or any of his brother's descendants, the curse will be upon his head. At the time we thought there were only three of us.''

''Your father must have known. Why didn't he acknowledge him formally?''

Rafi shrugged and smiled. ''Perhaps we will never know the answer to this. But there are some obvious possibilities.

''Jalal's birth was not legitimate, and in any case, he could only be at best fourth in line to the throne, because his father Aziz had died without ascending the throne. But in those early days the memory of the sheikh's first two sons was warm in the hearts of the people. Some might have wished to overlook Jalal's illegitimacy and hear my father name him heir. And my father already had three heirs and problems enough. This might have caused factions and rivalries…in any case, there was no possibility of certainty then. DNA testing did not exist, blood tests were inconclusive. I think my father did what was best.''

''But—''

''Yes. The real mystery is why, having done it, he never told us.'' Again Rafi shrugged. ''For this there is no obvious explanation. If one thing could be certain in all this, it was that Nusaybah would sooner or later break the embargo and tell her son his true parentage. She did this not long after we came into our full inheritance. Jalal sent petitions to us under the name Jalal ibn Aziz—Jalal son of Aziz—thinking we knew his name. When we ignored him…''

Hanifah entered with a tray of iced sorbet and tiny gold cups of Turkish coffee. Zara surfaced like a dog from water, shaking her head to clear it. As always when Rafi told her a story, she had lost track of time and surroundings.

"And what have you all decided to do for him?" She took a tiny spoonful of the lemony ice, a sip of coffee.

"We decided nothing. My mind was not on the task. They were united in closing the discussions and sending me back to my bride," he said softly, with a smile that would have melted her had she been stone. But she was not stone, she was flesh and blood and spirit, and so it set her on fire with love and longing.

"And now, my Beloved, this is our wedding night," he said, and rose to his feet before her.

Seventeen

He led her at last to the bedroom, where the doors were open onto the courtyard and soft mountain breezes stirred the white gauze drapes that created a haven around the big bed, a room within the room. Inside they were safe, enclosed, private. A fan turned gently, high above. Lamps were softly alight on low tables, the bed turned down and ready.

She stood facing him, too moved to speak. Love like this told you all the secrets of the universe, yet you were apparently tongue-tied in the presence of the Lover. In those long tedious nights in Jalal's fortress, Rafi had told her stories of the Lover and the Beloved, and now he would tell her the best story of all.

His hands clasped her head, tilting it as he gazed into her black eyes. He bent and kissed her, and the explosion of sensation along her skin made her gasp. She whimpered her longing and felt his arms tighten around her.

When he lifted his mouth, he was shaking. He had always known it would be as much as he could stand, to hold her and make her his own. He took a deep breath to steady himself, lifting his hands first to one ear, and then the other, and removed her earrings. He kissed each earlobe and set the earrings down.

With a smile she pulled her narcissus-bloom hair to one side and turned her back. He bent to bury his face in those perfumed curls. ''How many nights I have dreamed of this,'' he whispered passionately, sending shivers and thrills of matching desire through her. Oh, when you truly loved, how everything was changed! All charged with joy.

He removed her necklace and kissed the neck left bare by its removal. Then her cheek, her ear, her throat, and so turned her to face him again. He kissed her face, and everywhere electricity leapt between her skin and his lips, shocking and igniting them both.

His mouth passionately covered hers, his arms embraced her, her arms enwrapped his head. His hands stroked her, pressed her, flicked her, licked her, burned her as if he were flame and she…the phoenix, burned and renewed with each touch.

He found the tab of her zipper and drew it down the length of her back, his hand hungrily tracing the skin beneath all the way down. He leaned away from her and pulled the tunic down to reveal her breasts and her arms, and it fell to the floor around her feet. He found the fastening of the trousers, and they slipped down her silken legs, and she stood in a creamy silk thing like the bathing suit she had worn when he had first seen her and known his fate.

He closed his eyes. ''Your beauty would strike down mountains,'' he breathed. Then he lifted her bodily out of the silky pile of her clothes and slippers, an arm behind her back and under her knees, and stared down at her with eyes so hungry she was fainting.

''What if I had done this that day?'' he asked. ''What if I had climbed up to you in the waterfall and kissed you then, as I wished to do? What if I had lifted you and set you down—''

He set her down on the bed and lay beside her. His hand traced the line of the top of the little camisole, sending shivers of longing through them both. ''What would you have done?''

She remembered the shock she had felt, seeing him astride his beautiful horse, virile and unbelievably handsome, and staring at her with those hungry black eyes...there had been men with him, but if he had been alone, if he had come upon her there...

''I thought you were a bandit,'' she whispered.

''Yes, you thought I was a bandit! I saw fear in your eyes, but something else, too. I wished my Companions at the ends of the earth that morning! I said to myself, if I were alone, she would not say no to me. She would have run only to be chased and captured. She would have said yes in the end. Was it true?''

The way she was feeling now, the way she had felt every time he touched her...how could she have gone on saying no if he had touched her, pleaded with her? She smiled at the thought, the smile glinting up at him under her lashes, and his body leapt against hers.

''You were mine even then. Even believing I was a dangerous bandit—say it!''

''I was yours the first moment I looked at you,'' she whispered.

His mouth kissed hers with desperate hunger, and when she arched against him it lifted and found her breast through the warm silk, found the nipple, the soft underarm, and so upwards to her shoulder. He pulled one thin strap of her camisole out of the way of his kisses while his hand cupped her hip, her back, moved down her thigh.

He stood then, and threw off his own clothes, revealing the powerful chest, the slender waist, the muscled thighs and lastly...his strong, hungry sex.

She moaned helplessly and looked away.

"One day we will go back to the waterfall," he said, stretching out beside her on the wide, luxurious bed and beginning to stroke her again. "You will stand in it, all unknowing, and I will ride up on Raksh, and see you there. And I will climb up to you and enter—" he swallowed, helpless now with the desire and passion that stormed between them "—the water, and if you run away I will catch you and bring you back as I wished to do that day, and then I will undress you, so—"

With wildly trembling hands now, he lifted her upper body against his and began to draw the pale silk from the warmer, creamier silk of her skin, all the way down her long body. His breath brushed her throat, even that touch too much for her senses, so that she moaned and whimpered with hunger, need...and just a little with the fear of so much passion between them.

He closed his eyes as the action of his hands revealed her body to him. He had undressed her once before, but then, then he had put an iron guard on his wishes and his blood. Now there was nothing between what he wanted and what was right, now these two things were the same.

His passion was merciless. His hand stroked her breasts, her body. His mouth and tongue followed, he felt the heat of her mouth against his own skin, and then there was no boundary between him and her, there was only heat and honey and melting into one another. There was joy and passion and tenderness and a terrible terrible longing like the thirst of lifetimes assuaged.

He lay looking down at her, her face of unimagined beauty—yet he had dreamed of it—and thought that to lie in the lap of the Beloved, to sip the flower's nectar, like the hummingbird, to burn like a moth on the candle's flame—this was the end of all seeking.

He thought so, even as the other seeking burned up in him, and he lifted himself and pushed there again, to that place where longing ceased, and then again, and again....

She moaned with the unimagined pleasure of each stroke

reaching its limit in her, knocking at some door within, demanding an opening, an answer. She wandered fainting through rooms of bright colour, past trees laden with fruit, tasting wine and honey. Sensation poured across all the senses, confusing them, so that she drank gold and silver light and heard honey and smelled heat, and saw Rafi's face in the centre of all, passionate, anguished, his eyes drunk with love.

"This is love," she said, making the momentous discovery.

"It is love," he echoed, and each knew that love was the melting together of all the senses, of reason, feeling, dreams, everything, to find paradise.

Deep, deep in her being, a door opened then, onto a world so magic she cried her surprise and joy from everything she was. He heard the cry, and then he, too, was released to enter that world.

For impossibly long, awe-filled moments of joy and sorrow, creation and destruction, night and day, being and not being, they experienced the great and terrible knowing that is Union. They smiled and wept, and cried out and were silent, and knew and did not know, and were and were not, Love.

Epilogue

"Well, Marta, this is getting to be a habit," said Barry.

Marta smiled broadly into camera two. "Yes, indeed, Barry! It's been quite a year for the Barakat Emirates! The princes, it seems, have the knack of pulling absolute triumph out of the jaws of disaster!"

"But losing your chance with all three of the princes in one day, Marta, that must be hard."

"They might have spared a thought for all the women in the world they were going to disappoint, all getting married on the same day! But you know, there's hope. I've been taking a good look at some of those—what are they called?—Cup Companions to the princes, that's sort of like the Order of the Garter or something, I understand, and they're a pretty handsome crew."

Barry lifted his hand to the earphone. Just then the screen was filled with the image of a massive arched portico magnificently decorated in the painted blue tiles and calligraphic inscriptions of another century.

"Andrea, you're there?" said Barry's voice.

The camera panned down to the reporter, standing under the arch beside one of the beautiful columns.

"Yes, I'm here, Barry, outside the wonderful palace of Queen Halimah, here in Barakat al Barakat, the capital of the Emirates, where the weddings are about to take place. The princes chose the palace so that people of all faiths could attend the ceremony. Just before the ceremony starts we'll take you to the view inside the great Hall of Justice. According to tradition, it's the largest Hall of Justice ever built by any monarch anywhere. And apparently it's just about big enough to fit in all the guests who have clamoured to come here today from all around the world.

"As you've seen over the past hour that they've been arriving, we have numerous heads of state, and representatives of royal families, crowned and uncrowned, as well as a massive representation of the aristocracy and the ordinary folk of all three Emirates, and lots of the world's idle rich. Of course huge delegations from the families of the brides. There are Barakati artists, writers and poets, many of whom will feel moved to record their impressions of the event, and even a few lowly representatives of the press.

"They are all seated, and the ceremony is about to begin. We're told that the ceremony will draw on both the Barakati and the Western traditions in a unique service used only on this occasion, because, as it says here, let me get this right…" She lifted a paper and read, "'Because, although God may be worshipped in many different ways and in numerous different guises, and his message has been brought by a variety of prophets, He is always and ever One.'"

"I like that," said Marta. "No wonder the place is called Blessed."

"I hear we'll be going to the ceremony in about a minute, Andrea. Anything to add before we go?" Barry intervened.

"Just a few statistics—the three princes have chosen three very different wives, although all are native English speakers. Caroline Langley, Prince Karim's bride, as we all remember, is an American, and she's a blonde. She was born into old money, but when her family lost its wealth, she turned to selling clothes in a designer boutique. Jana Stewart is British—a Celt, she insists, and with the red hair to prove it. She's Prince Omar's choice. She was born to the purple, but turned her back on privilege to become a teacher in an underprivileged area of London. And Zara Blake, the hostage whom Prince Rafi rescued and then proposed to, is a black-haired Canadian with a little bit of everything in her heritage. She's an archaeologist with the team that discovered the lost city of Iskandiyar not so long ago in East Barakat. That's how she and Prince Rafi—"

"We're going inside, Andrea," Marta interrupted, "where the ceremony is about to start. We'll get back to you."

As the massive doors opened, an expectant hush fell over the congregation. There was a pause several heartbeats long, and then the magnificent Princes of Barakat entered the great Hall of Justice through the massive doorway, three abreast.

Those who were watching took a breath. With natural dramatic flair, the princes paused for a moment. Their costumes were magnificent, but no more than was matched by their own regal bearing and proud nobility. Pearls, precious gems, silk and gold embroidery adorned their masculinity like a second skin, so naturally did it become them.

All three smiled and flicked glances among themselves when they saw the throng who had come to help them celebrate their weddings. The Hall of Justice, that had once teemed with those seeking redress, was a long hall divided into three by two rows of intricately decorated pillars. Each of the three sections now had an aisle created between the temporary seats, running from the massive doors at the end of the room all the way to the raised dais at the other end, where the princes stood.

Except for those three aisles, the hall was jammed with people. Rows and rows of chairs seemed to run into infinity.

The princes smiled and nodded, then proceeded solemnly to the centre of the dais, where the priest awaited them at the long altar which had been set up underneath a beaten gold canopy. Behind them, through the doors, came all thirty-six of their Cup Companions. Usually the Companions drew lots at ceremonial occasions, but this time none would be denied his rightful part in the proceedings.

"Have you ever seen so much masculine splendour all in one place?" Marta murmured to the viewers in an awed hush, as the Companions lined up along the edge of the podium, spacing themselves to fill the whole width of the hall. Then, at a signal, they moved in unison down the steps to stand facing the congregation.

The Companions were almost as magnificent as the princes they served. Each wore a richly coloured turban and a ceremonial sword, and around his neck a jewel on a pearl rope, the symbol of their high office.

There was music playing somewhere, but it was impossible to be certain what instruments were played. Flutes, perhaps, and rebecks, and tambourines.

Two Companions from each group detached themselves and strode in pairs down each of the three aisles to the great entrances at the other end of the hall.

There was another long hush of expectation, and then the three pairs of doors were opened. Through each of them, with measured steps, came one of the three brides, Jana Stewart for Prince Omar, Caroline Langley for Prince Karim, and Zara Blake for Prince Rafi.

All wore the traditional Western white, but each dress was individual, and each bride had chosen a different colour for her flowers.

The first that the cameras picked up wore a dress that

was closest to the Eastern *shalwar kamees*. It bore a high neck, was open in a V at the front, had long full sleeves buttoned tightly at the wrist, and fell to mid-calf. Underneath were the flowing trousers in the same white on white brocaded silk. On her feet she wore delicately strapped shoes with heels. She carried ruby red and white roses in her bouquet, with a thousand tiny red and white rosebuds threaded all through her luscious dark hair, as though each curl held a flower.

"Princess Zara," murmured Marta, to any member of the television audience who might happen to have spent the past month in a coma.

The second bride wore a long, slim, elegant outfit, with sleeves to the elbow, unwaisted. A gored coat, with a stiff high-standing lace ruffle running behind her neck and down into the cutaway bodice to give her outfit an Elizabethan air, was open over a matching shift beneath. She carried a white-and-green bouquet, deep-coloured ivy and the white hawthorn of her homeland falling from her waist to the floor in thick, fertile profusion. Her tawny hair was crowned with a wreath of ivy.

"And Princess Jana."

The third bride was veiled. She wore a romantic dress, flounce upon flounce of silk lace over a thick crinoline, and above, a smooth snug bodice and tiny sleeves. She carried a spilling bouquet of blue flowers of different varieties and hues, and the veil that hid her face trailed several yards behind her.

"And Princess Caroline," murmured Marta.

As if the world didn't already know.

Behind each bride came her attendants. Like their grooms, each bride had twelve. Each had chosen to be attended by a mix of ages, from three to thirty. Some carried bouquets, some overflowing baskets, but the message of female youth and beauty was there. They spilled behind their own bride with little rhyme or pattern, wearing her colour, ruby, green, blue, in a span of shades and tones.

The congregation smiled and shook their heads in amazed delight.

It was a long walk to the altar. The Companions who had opened the doors closed them again and followed the brides and their attendants back to the front of the hall. When they got there, all the bridesmaids stopped at the lowest level, in front of the handsome Cup Companions.

Each one went to a different Companion, except for one tiny stalwart beauty with long golden curls and a blue dress who climbed determinedly up the steps behind Caroline Langley and followed her all the way to the altar. Looking down, Caroline smiled approvingly through her veil and then had eyes only for Prince Karim, waiting there for her.

Lena, dressed in shot rose silk, accompanied Zara. And Jana's young sister, dressed in forest green, smiled tremulously as she followed Jana to where dark-eyed Omar waited.

"The princes drew lots to establish the order of their vows," Marta informed her audience, though the same information had already been aired many times in the papers and on television in the run-up to this moment. "No one except themselves will know what that order is until we see it happen. And now, from this moment until the service is over, there is to be no commentary."

All the commentators dutifully fell silent as the service began. It was a mixture of hymns and readings, sermons and songs, music and dance. The vows of each bride and groom were taken in turn. Young bridesmaids yawned and dropped their flower baskets, the older women in the congregation wept a few tears, the Companions exchanged warm dark looks with the older bridesmaids.

In short, as is fitting at a wedding, everyone did pretty much as nature dictated.

And then it was over. Bells rang, music played, and the Princes of Barakat embraced their new brides.

"Prince Rafi of East Barakat, as we all know, was married some time ago," Marta reminded her viewers. "For him and Princess Zara this was really more like a blessing. But the others waited for the official moment. There's Princess Caroline, without her veil now, of course. Blue flowers in her hair, as well, I see.''

The congregation was on its feet now. All the brides and grooms were still in the Hall of Justice, as were the Companions and attendants. This was as planned. ''They'll move to the Throne Room now, where the reception is being held,'' Barry informed all those who had not heard the details before.

''Yes, there are Prince Omar and Princess Jana looking over their shoulders...they're leading the way down the central aisle, and then it will be out into the sunshine, where they'll greet the waiting crowds, and the whole party will cross the courtyard...yes, there go Princes Rafi and Karim and their new princesses...the sunshine is spilling into the room through the doors....

''What a fabulous day!'' said the announcer.

* * * * *

Silhouette® SPECIAL EDITION®
AND SILHOUETTE®
Desire®
The Bachelor Bet

In bestselling author **Joan Elliott Pickart's** *engaging
new series, three bachelor friends have bet that
marriage and family will never be a part of their lives.
But they'll learn* never *to bet against love....*

TAMING TALL, DARK BRANDON
Desire#1223, June 1999
Brandon Hamilton had long ago given up on the idea of
home, hearth and babies. But when he meets stubborn beauty
Andrea Cunningham, he finds himself in danger of being
thoroughly and irrevocably tamed....

THE IRRESISTIBLE MR. SINCLAIR
Special Edition #1256, July 1999
Taylor Sinclair believes marriage is for fools, but he
reconsiders when he falls for Janice Jennings—a secretly
stunning woman who hides behind a frumpy disguise. A
barrier Taylor vows to breach...

THE MOST ELIGIBLE M.D.
Special Edition #1262, August 1999
She's a woman without a past. He's a man without a future.
Still, **Dr. Ben Rizzoli** cannot quell his passion for the delicate
amnesiac who's made him live and love—and long for the
family he believes he can never have....

Don't miss **Joan Elliott Pickart's** *newest series,*
***The Bachelor Bet**— in Silhouette Desire
and Silhouette Special Edition!*
Available at your favorite retail outlet.

Silhouette®

If you enjoyed what you just read,
then we've got an offer you can't resist!

Take 2 bestselling love stories FREE!

Plus get a FREE surprise gift!

*This June 1999, the legend
continues in Jacobsville*

Diana Palmer

LONG, TALL TEXANS
EMMETT, REGAN & BURKE

This June 1999, Silhouette brings readers
an extra-special trade-size collection
for Diana Palmer's legion of fans.
These three favorite Long, Tall Texans
stories have been brought back in
one collectible trade-size edition.

*Emmett, Regan & Burke are about to be led
down the bridal path by three irresistible women.
Get ready for the fireworks!*

Don't miss this collection of favorite
Long, Tall Texans stories…
available in June 1999
at your favorite retail outlet.

Then in August 1999 watch for
LOVE WITH A LONG, TALL TEXAN
a trio of brand-new short stories featuring
three irresistible Long, Tall Texans.

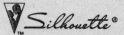

SILHOUETTE® Desire®

A hidden passion, a hidden child, a hidden fortune.

Revel in the unfolding of these powerful, passionate…

SECRETS!

A brand-new miniseries from Silhouette Desire® author

Barbara McCauley

July 1999
BLACKHAWK'S SWEET REVENGE (SD #1230)
Lucas Blackhawk wanted revenge! And by marrying Julianna Hadley, he would finally have it. Was exacting revenge worth losing this new but true love?

August 1999
SECRET BABY SANTOS (SD #1236)
She had never meant to withhold the truth from Nick Santos, but when Maggie Smith found herself alone and pregnant, she had been unable to face the father of her child. Now Nick was back—and determined to discover what secrets Maggie was keeping.…

September 1999
KILLIAN'S PASSION (SD #1242)
Killian Shawnessey had been on his own since childhood. So when Cara Sinclair showed up in his life claiming he had a family—and had inherited millions—Killian vowed to keep his loner status. Would Cara be able to convince Killian that his empty future could be filled by a shared love?

Secrets! available at your favorite retail outlet store.

SILHOUETTE®
Desire®

COMING NEXT MONTH

#1225 PRINCE CHARMING'S CHILD—Jennifer Greene
10ᵗʰ Anniversary Man of the Month/Happily Ever After
Pregnant? Impossible! Nicole Stewart knew she hadn't done *anything*
that could get her pregnant! Of course, she did have some passionate
memories of being in handsome architect Mitch Landers's strong
arms.... But that had been a dream...right?

#1226 LOVERS' REUNION—Anne Marie Winston
Explorer Marco Esposito's knee—and career—were shot, but he
was determined to discover new territories again. Then beauty
Sophie Morrell walked back into his life. Sophie had always loved
Marco, but could she convince him that *she* was his most exciting
*re*discovery?

#1227 THAT McCLOUD WOMAN—Peggy Moreland
Texas Brides
He was determined to protect his heart. Jack Cordell had been
hurt deeply once, and even though he was attracted to lovely
Alayna McCloud, he would never again bare his soul to another. It
was up to Alayna to show Jack that with love anything is possible....

#1228 THE SHEIK'S SECRET—Judith McWilliams
Being mistaken for his twin brother was the plan. Falling in love with
his brother's ex-fiancée *wasn't!* Yet how could Sheik Hassan Rashid
resist Kali Whitman's tempting sensuality? But would Kali's love
endure once she learned Hassan was not the man he claimed to be?

#1229 PLAIN JANE'S TEXAN—Jan Hudson
It was love at first sight. At least for millionaire Matt Crow.
But plain-Jane Eve Ellison needed some convincing. So Matt sat down
in his boardroom to plan a campaign to win her heart. But Eve had
other ideas...and they didn't involve a boardroom....

#1230 BLACKHAWK'S SWEET REVENGE—Barbara McCauley
Secrets!
Lucas Blackhawk wanted revenge! And by marrying Julianna Hadley, he
would finally have it. But Lucas soon discovered that sweet Julianna
was nothing like her cold family. Was exacting revenge worth losing
this new but true love?